SWEET SURPRISE

The second Casey burst through the door of her suite, she knew something was wrong. Most of her suitemates were sitting on the couch or floor of the lounge, throwing her funny, quizzical glances.

"Okay," Casey said, hands on hips. "What gives?"

"Oh, nothing," Reva said blithely.

Stephanie sniffed. "You sure have him wrapped around your finger."

Casey cocked her head. "Who?"

Eileen grinned. "Charley!"

"Charley? But he's in—" Casey started to say, then crossed the lounge in three long strides. Her door was open a crack, and she pushed her way in.

"Charley!" she cried, her jaw dropping.

"Hi, Case," he said casually, as if he hadn't just come all the way from California. "Aren't you happy to see me?"

NANCY DREW ON CAMPUS™

Available from ARCHWAY Paperbacks

Nancy Drew
on campus™ # 10

Party Weekend

Carolyn Keene

AN ARCHWAY PAPERBACK
Published by POCKET BOOKS
New York London Toronto Sydney Tokyo Singapore

This book is a work of fiction. Names, characters, places and incidents are products of the author's imagination or are used fictitiously. Any resemblance to actual events or locales or persons, living or dead, is entirely coincidental.

AN ARCHWAY PAPERBACK *Original*

An Archway Paperback published by
POCKET BOOKS, a division of Simon & Schuster Inc.
1230 Avenue of the Americas, New York, NY 10020

Copyright © 1996 by Simon & Schuster Inc.
Produced by Mega-Books, Inc.

ISBN: 0-671-52758-4

First Archway Paperback printing June 1996

10 9 8 7 6 5 4 3 2 1

NANCY DREW, AN ARCHWAY PAPERBACK and colophon are registered trademarks of Simon & Schuster Inc.

NANCY DREW ON CAMPUS is a trademark of Simon & Schuster Inc.

Cover photos by Pat Hill Studio

Printed in the U.S.A.

IL 8+

CHAPTER 1

Sky blue eyes sparkling, Nancy Drew took a big breath and raised her eyes from the playing cards in her hand.

"I'll see your two and raise you another three," she said, tossing some poker chips on the growing mound in the middle of the card table.

Jake Collins, her boyfriend, sighed dramatically and spread his cards facedown. "You're too much for me, Drew. I fold."

Nancy leaned back in her seat and looked around the Zeta fraternity house lounge at the Kappa women and other Wilder University students gathered around the card tables. They were all there to help the Zetas practice blackjack and poker so they could be dealers at the upcoming

Black & White Nights Casino Fund-raising Weekend.

The benefit would start off on Friday night with a five-hundred-dollar-a-ticket black-tie affair for organizing committee members, alumni, faculty, and trustees. Saturday night the casino would be open to anyone, including students, for a fifteen-dollar donation. All the door money and the profits from the gambling tables would go to various on-campus charitable organizations.

Nancy couldn't believe how perfectly the planning had gone so far. Her best friend Bess Marvin had arranged for the popular campus band the Beat Poets to play. And Bess's friend Brian Daglian and Nancy's famous, former TV star suitemate, Casey Fontaine, had put together a hilarious "lounge act." One of Wilder U's biggest donors, H. Samuel Porter, had not only agreed to be honorary chairperson of the Black & White Nights Alumni Committee but had also put up the money for the casino "bank"—five thousand dollars.

After kicking his cowboy boots up on the card table, Jake grabbed a couple of pretzels from a bowl near his poker chips and tossed them into his mouth.

"Hey! You're eating my stash!" Bess complained. She peered down at her cards and tugged at a stray lock of blond hair, scrunching up her face in deep thought.

"If you don't make your bet soon," Paul Cody, Bess's boyfriend, warned, *"I'm* going to eat your whole pretzel stash!"

"Mmmm, someone's getting a little testy about his rapidly shrinking pile of chips," quipped Eileen O'Connor, another of Nancy's suitemates.

Flipping back a stray reddish blond curl, Nancy grinned at Paul. He'd lost most of his chips in the first two rounds.

"What's so funny?" he asked, catching Nancy grinning at him.

"Just that you're on the organizing committee for Black and White Nights, in charge of the gambling tables, and you're such a lousy card player," Nancy said.

Paul fired back a mock glare. "Do you see all the people in this room? Well, I taught them everything they know."

"That's what I was afraid of," wisecracked Holly Thornton, one of Bess's Kappa sisters, as she strolled by.

"Shh!" Bess said, waving her away. "I'm thinking."

Nancy drummed her fingers on the table. "It's only practice, Bess," she murmured. "What happens when we start betting with *real* money tomorrow night?"

"Okay, okay, I'm ready," Bess said, not taking her eyes off her cards. "Okay. I'll see your bet. What have you got?"

Nancy set her cards down—three twos and a pair of kings. "Full house."

"Nancy!" Bess moaned. "That's not fair. You *always* beat me!"

Bess put down her cards.

"But you only had a pair of queens," Paul said, pointing. "You're not even close."

Bess shrugged. "So I was bluffing."

Paul leaned in and planted a kiss on her cheek. "Be careful at the blackjack tables tomorrow," he said.

As Nancy swept her winnings toward her stack, she felt her knee being tickled softly under the table. She looked up to catch Jake winking at her.

"This weekend's going to be great," he said quietly. "Everyone's done a terrific job."

"I just hope a lot of people show up tomorrow," Paul said.

"Why wouldn't they?" Nancy asked.

"Five hundred dollars for one ticket is a ton of money," Bess answered for him.

"Not for our board of trustees," Jake replied coolly. "And there are plenty of Wilder alumni who are loaded, too."

"I'm dying to see Casey and Brian's lounge act," Holly said excitedly, changing the subject.

"Speaking of entertainment," Nancy spoke up. "Bess has become quite the party planner."

Blushing, Bess playfully slapped at Paul's hand as it drifted toward the bowl of pretzels. "I just

4

hope I win a little money this weekend," Bess announced to everyone.

"It'll be fun to be able to win real money," Holly said.

"Just as long as no one wins *too* much," Paul said. "We want most of it to get to the charities."

Nancy glanced quickly at Jake. As much as she was enjoying herself, Nancy didn't exactly want to spend the rest of the evening in a lounge full of other students. The weekend was going to be hectic, without much time for romance, and all she wanted right now was to be alone with the tall, brown-haired junior sitting to her left.

Nancy made a big show of yawning. "I think I'm going to call it a night," she said, nudging Jake under the table with her knee.

"What? Oh, me, too," Jake agreed, stretching his arms over his head.

Bess crossed her arms. "Yeah, right."

Nancy and Jake stood up, and Nancy snatched the last pretzel from Bess's bowl, leaving only salt and crumbs. "For the road," Nancy mumbled, taking a bite and giving a little wave.

"What *is* that?" Stephanie Keats asked as she draped her slinky body over the couch in the lounge of Thayer Hall, Suite 301, and stared down at a group of her suitemates sitting cross-legged on the floor.

Reva Ross, Kara Verbeck, Casey Fontaine, and Liz Bader were playing cards.

"It's called casino," Casey explained enthusiastically. "Kind of a cross between go fish and bridge."

"Why don't you join us?" Reva asked, shifting to straighten her white flannel nightgown.

"Are you kidding?" Stephanie sneered. "It looks *spectacularly* dull."

"Suit yourself," Liz replied, slapping down a card. "It's good practice for this weekend, though."

Stephanie waved her away. "Yeah, right."

"So," Reva said between hands, "what are you guys wearing Saturday night?"

"I was thinking of my long, blue shimmery dress," Casey tossed out.

"The one you wore to the TV awards last year?" Kara asked.

"Well, *I'm* wearing silver and white," Reva announced. "All sheer and clingy."

Kara fanned herself. "Whew, sounds sexy. Andy's going to melt."

"Speaking of Andy," Reva said soberly, "the guy who fixes our computers came by today. He asked me out again."

"Is he good-looking?" Stephanie asked blithely.

"What's the difference?" Reva challenged.

Stephanie examined her nails. "It makes all the difference in the world."

"I just want him to get the message once and for all that I'm not interested," Reva said. "I don't want to hurt his feelings, though. He's such a nice guy."

"Ask Stephanie for some advice," Casey suggested. "She's a professional at getting rid of guys."

"I said I *didn't* want to hurt his feelings," Reva replied.

"Don't play *that* card," Stephanie said to Kara, ignoring Casey and Reva. "Play *this* one." Leaning over, she tugged the ten of spades out of Kara's hand to take the ten of diamonds.

"I thought you didn't know how to play, Steph," Liz said.

Stephanie shrugged. "You don't have to be a rocket scientist to figure it out."

"Well, good going, Kara," Liza said, adding up the points. "You won."

"I did?" Kara looked surprised.

As they were picking up, Casey sighed audibly. "Charley's coming up for a visit in a couple weeks, but it feels like it's *years* away still."

"The question is," Reva said with mock seriousness, "can you tear yourself away from casino long enough to hang out with him?"

"Hmmm," Casey said, a slow smile tugging at the corners of her mouth. "Good point."

"Maybe Stephanie can amuse him for you," Liz suggested.

"Any time," Stephanie said in her sultriest voice.

"In your dreams," Casey shot back good-naturedly. After a second she added, "I know what I'll do—I'll teach Charley how to play casino. That way I won't have to choose between him and the game!"

As the grandfather clock in the hallway of Zeta house chimed eleven, Paul checked out the list of assignments he'd taped up to the wall. Beside each assignment was the name of a Zeta brother.

"Let's see," he muttered to himself: "Roulette, blackjack, poker, craps— Okay, all the tables are covered." He turned to two frat brothers. "Mike, you and Bob are the gatekeepers. Controlling the door is the most important job."

Paul looked toward the corner where two offensive linemen on the W.U. football team were stretched out on couches.

"So let's hear it," Paul said, cupping his ear.

Bob and Mike cleared their throats and repeated Paul's orders: "People under eighteen can't get in unless they can prove they're Wilder students. All people twenty-one and over get a stamp on the back of their hands so they can drink at the bar."

"Does alcohol leave the bar?" Paul quizzed.

Bob and Mike obediently shook their heads.

Eileen, settled deep in an overstuffed couch, cleared her throat. "Last week you said that if the Kappas won more money than the Zetas this weekend, you guys would take us all out to a fancy dinner."

A bunch of Zetas started laughing. "Dream on!"

Eileen and Bess exchanged smug looks.

"*If* you win more money," Paul said, grinning mischievously, "and that's a big if—we'll consider it."

Eileen crossed her arms. "Not good enough."

"Only if you promise to take *us* out when *we* win," one of the Zetas piped up.

Eileen's eyes flashed. "You're on."

Paul glanced at his watch. I almost forgot! he thought. "Speaking of money—and charity," he said, eyeing Bess and Eileen, "I have to go see Porter to go over money stuff."

"How much did you say each table is getting?" Eileen asked.

"Five hundred," Paul replied.

"I sure hope we'll be able to pay him back his five grand," Bob remarked from the corner.

"We'll be able to pay him back," Paul said, smiling. "And then some. If everything goes according to plan, ticket sales on the first night alone should bring in more than fifty thousand."

"It's too bad Max isn't here to see all of our hard work pay off," Bess said sadly.

Max Krauser, the student coordinator of Helping Hands, the charity most involved in the Casino weekend, had flown home to California a few weeks before because his mother was dangerously ill.

"When Max gets back, I know he'll be pleased," Paul said proudly with a glint in his eye.

Bess crossed her arms, her lips pursed in mock suspicion. "I don't know, Cody. Can we trust you not to run off with the dough?"

Paul laughed, though part of him was caught off guard by the joke. He'd never stolen so much as a piece of bubble gum in his life, but he had to admit that some small part of him had wondered what it would be like to have a lot of money all at once.

Paul threw Bess a big wink. "You can trust me, don't worry."

As Nancy and Jake strolled hand in hand across the quad, Nancy shivered in the crisp evening air. Jake wrapped an arm around her shoulders and pulled her tightly toward him.

Everything's so perfect, Nancy thought. Her breath puffed out in little gray clouds that mingled with Jake's. The Milky Way stretched above them like a bright ribbon in the night. The quad was quiet; it was just two of them, alone.

"Happy?" Jake asked, reading her mind.

"Excited—and nervous," Nancy replied. Her heart *was* pounding, though she couldn't tell if it was because of the weekend or Jake. They'd been going out for a few weeks now, and he still made her heart gallop and her palms sweat.

"I just hope everything goes according to plan," she said.

Out of the corner of her eye, Nancy saw a shooting star streaking across the sky. "Look!" she said, pointing. "Oh. It's already gone." The star disappeared before Jake had a chance to see it.

"Sometimes good things don't last," Jake mused out loud.

Nancy frowned. "What's that supposed to mean?"

"It means that you have to take advantage of every moment," Jake said softly. He took Nancy's face in his hands and bent down to kiss her. Nancy wrapped her arms around Jake's waist and leaned in against his chest. She could hear his heart racing, too. With his breath on her lips and his strong back beneath her fingertips, everything about him felt right. She closed her eyes as his lips met hers in a gentle kiss.

"Hey, I thought you guys were going to *sleep*," a voice called to them from out of the night.

Jake let go of Nancy and stepped back. The voice belonged to Bob, one of Paul's Zeta brothers, jogging by.

"Um, we are," she replied. "What are *you* doing out so late?"

"I'm on my way to the Hot Truck to get a few subs for the guys," Bob said, panting.

"Those Zeta guys never stop eating," Nancy said, leaning back into Jake. But the magic of the moment had been broken.

As soon as Bob jogged off, Nancy said, "Maybe we'll have better luck this weekend."

"You can bet on it," Jake said good-naturedly as they continued walking to Thayer. "By the way, when is Helping Hands going to assign you a little sister?"

Nancy shrugged. She was excited about getting involved with a little sister. The girl would be a teen from a single-parent home. Wilder students spent time each week with their little sisters or brothers and became friends and role models for the kids. Nancy hadn't yet been matched up with anyone. "All the girls already have big sisters. They're waiting until a new girl comes into the program."

"Well, whoever it is will be one lucky young lady," Jake said.

Outside Thayer Nancy reached up and softly touched his cheek. "Speaking of lucky young ladies," she said, "there's one standing right here.

But she's going to drop from exhaustion any second."

"Not while I'm around to hold her up," Jake said. Before Nancy knew what was happening, Jake had lifted her up in his arms, kissed her softly, and carried her off to her dorm.

CHAPTER 2

Jake was waiting outside the door of Freddy's Tux and Formal Wear early the next morning when an old, stooped man walked up jangling a handful of keys. He was wearing out-of-date seventies polyester pants and a frayed cardigan sweater, not exactly an outfit to inspire confidence in someone shopping for a tux.

"You're a little early," the old man said to Jake as he pushed open the door. "I'm not quite open yet."

"Are you the owner?" Jake asked, following him into the dusty shop. Black tuxedo jackets and other formal wear flowed out into the room from the shelves and the racks.

"I'm Freddy," the old man replied, and peered

at Jake. "You're a last-minute customer," he said.

"How can you tell?" Jake asked, looking around.

Freddy smiled slightly. "You look worried."

Jake nodded. "I am worried."

The old man grinned triumphantly.

Jake had waited until the last day to get his tux for Black & White Nights. Nancy had reminded him every day for a week. And now, here it was, Friday morning, and he still had no tux. He was nervous and in a hurry.

"You need to impress a lady?" Freddy added.

Jake laughed. "You got it."

Freddy snapped a tape measure and walked toward Jake as if he were a strangler. "I specialize in last-minute customers," he boasted, "who need to impress ladies. I have just the thing."

Five minutes later Jake was standing in front of a three-way mirror. Freddy was picking at the shoulders and cuffs, getting them to fall just right. "Perfect," he said.

Jake eyed the suit, then leveled an investigative gaze at Freddy.

"You really think so?" he asked, incredulous. "You don't think a more modern tux would be better?"

Freddy gave him the okay sign. "This is the newest look. They call it 'retro.' It'll kill her."

But is that a good thing or a bad thing? Jake wondered.

"Well, okay, I'll take it—I guess," he said, permitting himself a tentative smile.

"It's the best one I have. The *last* best one, that is. All the rest are rented. It *is* the last minute," Freddy reminded Jake.

"You're right," Jake said, somehow not quite believing it. He turned left, then right, eyeing himself up and down. "I think."

As Jake left the store with the boxed tuxedo under one arm, and the box containing shoes, cuff links, and a bow tie in the other, he squinted into the clear morning. "I mean, a tux is a tux. How bad can it be? If this is what's 'in,' then I'll obviously look cool. Won't I?"

"Another doughnut?" Liz Bader called across the stage of Hewlitt Performing Arts Center to Daniel Frederick. Blowing a stubborn piece of short brown hair out of her eyes, she offered him his choice from one of the boxes of pastries she'd brought in that morning. But when Daniel lifted his head, she saw he was holding three nails between his teeth, a hammer in one hand, and a tape measure in the other.

Liz laughed. "I guess not right now."

Daniel mumbled something unintelligible.

"Hungry?" Liz guessed.

Daniel mumbled something else.

"Sure, whatever you say." Liz laughed again.

Daniel squinted, his mouth curling in a smile around the nails. Liz quickly looked away, suddenly self-conscious about the cutoff T-shirt and worn, tight blue jeans she'd accidentally-on-purpose put on that morning.

I have to admit, she thought to herself, *when Nancy asked me to work with Daniel on building the sets and games for Black & White Nights, I was positive it was too soon to be so close to him again.*

But they'd talked about how their budding romance had gone sour because of Daniel's involvement in a fraternity hazing incident. Things were finally smoothed over between them. Liz couldn't deny the little backflip her heart did whenever she got near Daniel now. While drawing up plans for the games tables and the giant photo cutouts, and the wheel of fortune, there'd been plenty of shoulder knocking and finger grazing. And they had even decided to go together to the black tie evening for Black & White Nights.

Liz glanced at Daniel again. In his jeans and sleeveless T-shirt, he definitely was cute.

Daniel sighed and stood up. Liz went back to applying the finishing touches to the giant wheel for their version of *Wheel of Fortune.* She'd just been writing the word *Jackpot!*

"How's it coming?" Daniel asked, moving silently up to her.

He was standing so close behind her that she could feel his breath on the back of her neck.

"Talk about last minute," she said, squinting as she concentrated. "There, done. What do you think?" she asked as she turned to him.

"Beautiful," Daniel replied softly.

Neither of them spoke for a minute. Liz could feel the tension rising. The air between them began to buzz electrically. She peered up at the giant wheel, as if it would tell her what to do next.

"Spin it!" she blurted out suddenly. "Let's give it a test whirl."

Daniel grabbed the wheel. He cleared his throat. "I know what *I'd* wish for," he said meaningfully. With his free hand he reached up and fingered a stray piece of hair that had fallen into Liz's eyes.

Liz could feel her heart racing. "Maybe it's time to get my hair trimmed," she said quietly. "It's driving me crazy."

"Me, too," Daniel replied, smiling.

"No . . . no . . . no . . . and no," Bess counted off as she tossed dresses and body suits over her shoulder one at a time. Most of her clothes lay in a heap behind her now.

Bess stepped back, surveyed the damage, and peered into her disorganized closet. "Nothing," she lamented. "I don't have a thing to wear tonight."

Her roommate, Leslie King, turned her eyes in Bess's direction. "That's too bad," she said mildly.

Leslie was hunched over her desk, marking passages in her biology textbook with a highlighter pen. Leslie was exact and meticulous, and usually Bess did something to aggravate her.

Until a few weeks ago, if Bess had so much as cleared her throat while Leslie was reading, Leslie would have flipped out. She was as straight as the unwrinkled chinos and oxford shirts she was fond of wearing, and as prim as her perfect ponytail.

But the fact was, the Ice Princess, bane of Bess's existence at Wilder, was starting to become a normal, more relaxed person. She'd been seeing a counselor since narrowly escaping being arrested for a murder a couple weeks before. When the police suspected Leslie of killing her professor, Bess was one of the few people who believed she was innocent. Leslie and Bess, once enemies, were more the Odd Couple now. In fact, Bess thought they were becoming friends.

"What about that red dress?" Leslie suggested.

Bess listened, a smile on her face. After all, Leslie *was* trying.

"Maybe for tomorrow night," Bess said, "the

funky student night. But tonight is black-tie only. Five hundred smackers a head."

Leslie cupped her chin in deep thought. "There'll be lots of rich, well-dressed adults," she murmured. "You'll have to be respectable, cultivated. Men in blue smokers—"

"Women in diamond tiaras?" Bess offered.

They both dissolved in laughter. Bess's eyes scanned Leslie's side of the room and came to rest on her roommate's closed closet door.

"Don't bother," Leslie said. "Everything in there is dry and boring. Big surprise, right?" Leslie asked, taking a shot at herself.

Bess reacted with surprise. She didn't know what to say. "It's not that," she replied quickly. Her mind had raced off in another direction: across campus toward Selena's, the popular downtown boutique that carried the latest in glamorous and tasteful.

She grabbed the phone and dialed George's number. When she got her answering machine, she hung up. Bess tried Nancy and Casey but got their machines, too.

"Who're you calling?" Leslie inquired, chewing on the top of her pen.

"I need a friend to come down to Selena's with me, but no one's around. And I really *hate* going there alone. I don't trust myself—"

Slowly Bess turned in Leslie's direction. Could she? Bess wondered. *Would* she? Leslie was lightening up, but did she actually have it in her to go on a shopping spree?

Leslie must have guessed what Bess was thinking because she wagged her head back and forth. "No way," she protested. "Not a chance. I have a huge bio exam Monday morning."

Bess grinned mischievously. "Monday's Monday, but today is today, which happens to be Friday. Live for the moment." Bess paused before adding, "In fact, I've always heard that shopping is therapeutic!"

It only took three seconds after Nancy remembered all her homework for her to forget it.

She was walking toward Hewlitt Performing Arts Center when out of the corner of her eye she spotted the roof of Wilder's Rockhausen Library, hovering behind a bank of red-gold trees on the far side of the quad. Nancy suddenly thought of all the late nights she was going to have to spend to catch up on her work. Then she pushed through the doors of Hewlitt and marched into the main hall where the casino was being set up. In less than a second all her worries vanished. She blinked, letting her eyes take in the transformation. Then she gasped.

"You guys are unbelievable!" Nancy said excitedly, dropping her knapsack holding the one textbook she was pretending she'd get a chance to look at today.

Liz, Holly, Eileen, and a few other students were moving from set to set with pots of touch-up paint. Paul was straightening stacks of chips and brushing at the green felt on the gaming tables. Daniel was on top of a tall stepladder, tying up a shimmering glass banquet hall. A dozen more students were roaming around sweeping and cleaning.

Taking it all in, Nancy was trying hard not to let her nervousness overwhelm her. The fact was, all their hard work organizing and planning had paid off. She stared at the wheel of fortune. "That's great, Liz. It looks just like the real thing."

"Is there a Nancy Drew here?" a voice called from the doorway. "I have a delivery from Collegetown Party Supply." A man in overalls was wheeling in a dolly stacked with boxes.

"Need a hand with all that, Nance?" Paul asked, wiping his hands on the sides of his pants.

"Thanks," Nancy said. "These boxes are heavy."

Nancy followed Paul down into the basement. It was like a maze, with hallways and more hallways branching in different directions. Everything was painted a dull gray, and none of the doors were marked. The light was dim, making it hard to see.

"It's a good thing we were able to get an entire storeroom to ourselves," Paul huffed, turning a final corner. "It's so confusing down here, we could easily have gotten our stuff mixed up with the Theater Department's things."

"No kidding," Nancy said. "I hope I don't get lost."

Finally Paul kicked open a door and dropped his box against the wall with the other party and gambling supplies.

"You think Max would be satisfied?" Paul asked, surveying the loot.

Nancy nodded. "I think everything looks great. And if we get the big crowd we're expecting," she said, "then Helping Hands and the other groups will get a lot of money."

Back upstairs, Nancy found George sitting on the edge of the small stage. "The next time I'm planning a party, remind me to come talk to you and your friends," George said, giving Nancy a friendly pat on the back.

"Well, your pasta party for the Earthworks ten-K run was awesome," Nancy replied.

George laughed. "Yeah, boiling water and opening boxes of spaghetti and jars of sauce was a real stretch!"

Nancy noticed Jake standing in the doorway, a fat grin on his face, and a big box tucked under each arm. Nancy's heart began to race at the thought of spending that night with him, all dressed up under a beautiful starry sky, with soft music leaking out of Hewlitt onto a patch of very private, very dark, grass outside.

Nancy eyed the boxes as Jake strolled over. He was raffishly handsome and intelligent and a talented journalist, but he wasn't exactly the world's sharpest dresser. She couldn't wait to see him dressed up in a gorgeous tux. She was dying to get a peek inside. "Let me see!" She snatched at the bigger box.

But Jake wouldn't let go. "Patience is a virtue."

Nancy and Jake exchanged challenging looks, but Jake still wouldn't let go.

"Tell me what it looks like," Nancy said.

Jake shook his head. "All I'll say is that you'll be pleasantly surprised."

CHAPTER 3

Casey stepped out of the Rockhausen Library and into the bright afternoon. The wide steps of the library were dotted with students, their faces tilted up to the sky in the low autumn sunlight. It was Friday afternoon, and the campus seemed to have heaved a collective sigh of relief—the weekend was officially on!

But Casey's mind wasn't on the weekend. It wasn't even at Wilder. Casey was still in nineteenth-century Russian literature.

"Wow," she muttered as she navigated the library steps between the clumps of chatting students. "Just a couple hours in a study carrel can feel like *forever.*"

Casey had never thought of herself as a workaholic—in anything but her acting, that is. But the paper she'd started for her Russian lit class was starting to obsess her.

Time to downshift, she reminded herself. She needed to get other things on her mind.

Like Brian. She was supposed to meet him at his dorm in an hour, grab something to eat at Java Joe's, then cruise over to Hewlitt to go through their lounge act one last time before tonight.

Casey hurried across campus toward Thayer Hall. She took the stairs up two flights two at a time and jogged toward her suite. But the second she burst through the door, she knew that something was wrong. Most of her suitemates were sitting on the couch or floor of the lounge, throwing Casey funny, quizzical glances.

"Okay," she said, hands on hips. "What gives?"

"Oh, nothing," Reva said blithely.

Stephanie sniffed. "You sure have him wrapped around your finger."

Casey cocked her head. "Who?"

Eileen grinned. "Charley."

"Charley? But he's in—" Casey started to say, then crossed the lounge in three long strides. Her door was open a crack, and she pushed her way in.

"Charley!" she cried, her jaw dropping.

Charley Stern smiled up at Casey from her

bed, where he was lying on his back with his shoes off, his hands behind his head. His dreamy dark eyes glistening, he opened his mouth in a wide grin, flashing her a row of pearly teeth.

"Hi, Case," he said casually, as if he hadn't just come all the way from California but had passed her in the hall a few minutes ago.

There were a thousand things Casey wanted to ask, but all she managed to get out was "What are you doing here?"

Charley sat up. "Aren't you happy to see me?"

Casey dropped down on the bed next to him and planted a warm kiss on his neck. "I'm always happy to see you," she said, though part of her wasn't so sure. Not right now, anyway. She had her performance tonight to think about and tomorrow night's performance and that Russian lit paper, and she had to keep studying for the exams coming up soon, and all her other work.

"But aren't we still going away during the three-day weekend in a few weeks?" she asked, suddenly worried that he was canceling their plans. She'd been looking forward to the break from school, especially since it would be after exams.

"Um, sure," Charley said hesitantly.

Casey gasped. A cold chill ran through her. "You're breaking up with me."

Charley leaped up and pulled Casey up into his arms. "Not in a million years. I just missed you."

And for a second Casey closed her eyes and let Charley do what he did so well: make her feel as if she were floating above the clouds. Her mind always traveled back to the first time she saw him, as her co-star on *The President's Daughter,* the TV show she'd starred in before going to Wilder. He was so handsome, he made her nervous and she fumbled her lines the entire first week of the show!

She felt Charley's soft fingers stroking the sides of her neck. His lips on hers, so soft and warm and safe. "It's great to see you," she said, melting into him.

"That flight from L.A. was really long," Charley said, rolling his neck.

"I know," Casey said, kneading his shoulders. "You must be tired—"

Suddenly she stepped back.

Disappointment deadened Charley's eyes. "What?"

"It's just—you have no idea what a busy time this is for me right now!" Casey said. "There's a huge charity thing tonight that Brian and I are performing at, and I'm already late to meet him to rehearse." She ran over to her dresser and started getting her things together.

Casey felt Charley's hands on her waist as he came up behind her, wrapping her in his strong arms. She felt his teeth nibbling at her neck. "But there's something I wanted to talk to you about," he said lovingly.

Casey clutched his hand and moved away. "Okay, Charley, but not right now. I'm really swamped, and—"

"It's something important," Charley cut her off.

Frustrated, Casey leaned on one hip and gazed at him. "I'm sorry, I just don't have the time now." She smiled stiffly. "Go get something to eat, and I'll find some time later, promise." Then she gently pushed him back, until she had him out the door, walking backward down the hall toward the lounge.

"This is *really* important," Charley protested.

"Later, Charley," Casey said as gently as she could. "I'm really glad you're here, but in less than an hour I have to look like Madonna!"

"Oh, Leslie," Bess said, trying to muster up some enthusiasm, "this one—it's, um, nice."

For the last hour Bess had been struggling to find the words to describe the dresses Leslie had been handing her over the dressing room door at Selena's. *Nice* was a common one, but *interesting* was definitely winning. The last thing Bess wanted to do was hurt Leslie's feelings. After all, she *did* ask her to come.

This dress was navy blue with big brass buttons

and wide, white lapels. Basically it made Bess look like her mother.

"It's very country club," Leslie insisted from the other side of the door. "Very proper."

Proper? Bess made a face in the mirror. Who wants to look proper? "Interesting," she said, and shuddered to imagine what Leslie's social life was like in high school.

"You hate it," Leslie concluded.

Bess winced. "I don't *hate* it exactly . . ."

She scanned the dressing room, looking for something to compliment. The small room was a jungle of discarded dresses. Clothes were everywhere, hanging off the hooks, draped over the door, flung high up over the wall.

I think I've tried on every piece of ugly clothing in the store, Bess thought. "I sort of like the flowered print dress," she said unconvincingly.

Silence. Leslie wasn't buying it.

Then Bess remembered the main rule for choosing someone to take shopping with you to pick out an outfit—you needed to have the same taste.

"Maybe bringing Leslie along wasn't such a hot idea," she muttered under her breath. But Selena's was closing in fifteen minutes. "Okay," she called cheerfully through the door, struggling not to show her frustration. "Think fun, think excitement. Think romance. Can you do that?"

Bess could practically hear the wheels churning

in Leslie's brain. Romance? she was probably wondering. What's that? Excitement?

A minute later Leslie was heaving over another navy blue outfit, this one with a long skirt. Bess slipped it over her arms and looked in the mirror. One word came blaring back at her. *"School-marm,"* she said.

"Then I guess you'll have to try this one," Leslie said, sighing, and flung something pale peach over the door. "It's one I didn't like—"

Which means I probably will, Bess thought to herself.

She quickly slipped it over her head and wriggled into it. Then she zipped it up and surveyed herself in the mirror.

The pastel peach color complemented her hair and complexion, and with its high waistline and little cap sleeves, the dress was a total knockout. Bess shook her head, and her golden hair shimmered in the light. The dress really made it glow and made her face radiate with light. "This one's *hot!*" she said. "Good find! Paul's going to love me in this."

"It's not really my idea of classy."

"But *romance,*" Bess said dreamily, pushing her way out of the dressing room. "Excitement."

Leslie looked Bess up and down and nodded slowly. "It does make you look terrific," she said, surprised.

Bess smiled at her roommate. "You have great taste after all."

"It was practically the last dress in the store," Leslie said. "I liked the other one better."

"The navy blue?" Bess looked at it, then at Leslie. A match made in heaven. "*You* try it on!"

Leslie scanned the dressing room, as if embarrassed that Bess could even suggest such a thing. "Me? I couldn't."

"Your mouth is saying no, no, no"—Bess laughed—"but your eyes are saying yes, yes, yes." Leaning in, she whispered conspiratorially, "Besides, in case you didn't know, it doesn't cost anything to try it on."

"But I don't need a new dress," Leslie insisted. "I'm not going to formal Black and White Nights."

"Believe me, Les," Bess said with an ironic smile, "with your closet, you *do* need a new dress. Besides, what about your therapy? Aren't you supposed to get out, and mingle, and make friends? And most of all, have *fun?*"

Leslie eyed the long navy blue dress hanging in Bess's dressing room. She studied her reflection in the mirror. "You really think it would look good?"

Bess grabbed the dress and pressed it into Leslie's hands. "Only one way to find out."

Leslie scowled, then gave up and sighed.

"Maybe you're right," she said, closing the dressing room door behind her. "I need to mingle."

Bess shook her head. Leslie needs some lessons in dressing, she thought to herself, but thank goodness, she's trying to become normal.

From the couch in Jake's living room, Nancy could hear Jake in the kitchen, knocking stuff around in the refrigerator. "Let's see what glorious refreshments *Chez* Jake has to offer today," he murmured. "Okay, listening? Flat soda, lemon juice, some old Chinese takeout, and"—Nancy could hear him shifting around an old pizza box—"week-old pizza crust. What'll it be?"

"Don't you or your roommates ever go shopping?" Nancy called.

"Shopping?" Jake replied. "What's that?"

Nancy shook her head. "Why have your own apartment if you don't cook?"

"So you and I have a place to be by ourselves?" Jake tried.

Nancy smiled. "Good answer," she said, then heard a pop and a fizz as Jake snapped open a can of soda. "What a clown," she said.

Jake appeared in the doorway, a syrupy smile on his face. "Anything to make you happy."

Nancy eyed the sealed tuxedo box sitting on the chair across the room. She was dying to see inside. But Jake was determined to surprise her.

It had been a Herculean struggle not to badger him about it.

But I can't take it anymore! she cried inwardly.

Jake slid down next to her, and Nancy started kissing his neck.

He cleared his throat. "Your soda's getting warm."

Nancy rubbed Jake's shoulders: a guaranteed way to butter him up. Just as he started to relax, Nancy whispered seductively in his ear, "Now, won't you let me take a look at your tux?"

Jake stiffened. "That's low. You know I can't deny you anything when you kiss my neck—"

"And rub your shoulders," Nancy added.

"And rub my shoulders," Jake agreed. "Well, okay. But *I* wanted it to be a surprise. I just want to get that out in the open."

Nancy leaped to her feet. "It will be! Promise. When you put it on, I'll pretend I never saw it." The box was wound in string three or four times, like a cake. "Where'd you get this, a bakery?"

Jake's eyes were glistening. He had a confident smile on his face.

"I bet it's gorgeous," Nancy said as she finally got the lid off. But when she held the tuxedo jacket up, she couldn't find anything to say. "Oh" was all she managed.

"You don't like it," Jake said disappointedly.

"It's not that I don't *like* it," Nancy quickly said. "I mean, the wide lapels are interesting and everything. And the cut is so, so retro. And the color, midnight blue, how unusual."

Jake looked surprised and concerned. Nancy wanted to say something nice, but all she managed was "It's an interesting choice—I guess. It's an original, anyway. Very retro."

"Right, that's what it's supposed to be, retro," Jake said.

Nancy was dubious.

"You hate it," Jake lamented.

Nancy covered her mouth to hide her laughter. She winced. "Only a little?"

Jake sighed. "The guy at the shop said this look was very 'in' right now."

Nancy grinned. "It might be, but it's not you."

Jake buried his face in his hands. "I *knew* it was weird."

Nancy lowered herself beside Jake and put her arm around his shoulders. "Look, it won't be so bad," she kidded, "just say you're in period costume."

Jake leaped to his feet. "That's it. It's going back."

Nancy swallowed a little laugh. She wasn't going to suggest it; she was going to let *him* do that. But she wasn't complaining, either.

With the box under his arm, Jake headed for the door. "Aren't you coming?" he asked.

Nancy wearily pushed herself up from the couch. She really would have liked an hour's nap.

But Jake had the take-no-prisoners look on his face.

"Of course I'm coming," she said.

Ten minutes later they were patiently waiting at the tux shop while Freddy was fitting a tux on a guy with a funny flip of black hair hanging in his eyes. *His* tux was normal: black, normal lapels, normal length. A simple black tux.

"Can you get one like that?" Nancy asked Jake in a lowered voice.

Jake shrugged. "I don't know, it is late." Jake cleared his throat. "I hope you have another one like that one," he said to Freddy.

Freddy looked up at Jake's box. "You don't like the tux?"

Nancy put her arms around Jake's shoulders. "His taste in women may be impeccable, but his taste in clothing leaves something to be desired," she teased. "It's a little *too* retro."

Nancy felt the point of Jake's elbow in her ribs. "It was his suggestion," Jake whispered.

Nancy quickly tried to cover. "Though of course *this* tuxedo—"

"Is the latest fashion trend," Freddy countered, irritated.

"Of course. Of course," Nancy said.

"It's just not what I needed for tonight," Jake said apologetically.

The guy with the hair flip cleared his throat. He was standing in front of the three-way mirror with one leg cuffed up to his hairy shin, and his sleeves hanging below his hands. "Could we finish please? I'm in a hurry."

Freddy looked Jake up and down. "I have only one modern tuxedo left," he said disapprovingly.

Before Jake opened his mouth, Nancy stepped forward. "He'll take it."

Freddy headed for a rack at the back of the store, picked up a tuxedo off a hanger, and handed it and a piece of paper to Jake.

"Fill this out. It is a waiver for the cufflinks and the studs. This one is much more expensive. You must sign—"

Nancy eyed the tuxedo. Classic black. She breathed a sigh of relief. "It's a deal."

CHAPTER 4

When Bess walked up to the entrance of Hewlitt, it was with the step of a woman who knew she looked beautiful. She could feel her new dress hug her. She knew that she'd caught the attention of many of the people mingling in the entranceway, drinking champagne from clear plastic glasses. She could feel their eyes evaluating her: the women's with envy, and the men's with admiration.

Paul was standing at the door with Bob, who was straining the seams of his tuxedo, waving the trustees and faculty through, dutifully checking the IDs of the few students with permission to attend that night. Inside, Bess could see Mike laughing with the trustees as they handed him their five-hundred-dollar donations.

Through the windows, she glimpsed the streamers and balloons and heard the jazzy funk music of the Beat Poets filtering out onto the lawn.

Even though Bess was involved in planning Black & White Nights, she still couldn't believe how great everything looked.

Including Paul.

Tall and lean, his hair combed off to the side, he looked as if he'd gotten a little sun. His face was tan, and his eyes sparkled like glass chips held up to the light.

"I can't believe that's him," she whispered to herself. "I mean, he's always attractive, but his tuxedo makes him gorgeous."

"You look spectacular," Paul said as Bess walked up. "I love that dress."

Bess smiled knowingly to herself. "Leslie helped me pick it out."

Paul froze in amused shock. "Your *roommate* Leslie?"

Bess nodded. "The very same."

Paul whistled. "Maybe I underestimated her."

"Maybe we all did," Bess said with a shrug. "But excuse me, Mr. Gorgeous, I think it's time you took my arm and escorted me inside."

As they passed Mike, Bess eyed the pile of checks and bills in the cashbox.

"I've never seen so much money in my life!" Mike whispered.

Paul looked worriedly at the money. Bess

knew he was about to say something like "Keep an eye on it" or "Be careful," but she snatched his hand and squeezed it, then raised her glossy lips to Paul's ear. "He has everything under control."

"Hang on a second. I just want him to know that I'm going to come empty the cashbox and bring the money downstairs every hour."

Paul had a quick word with Mike, who nodded, then whispered something in Paul's ear, which made Paul smile and relax.

"Satisfied?" Bess asked when Paul came back.

Paul laughed. "Mike, a human Fort Knox."

"Good," Bess said, "because *I* don't want you distracted from your most important task."

"And what might that be?" Paul asked.

Bess flashed him her warmest smile. "Me!"

Paul escorted her into the flow of the crowd, through the double doors. Some people were sitting at candlelit cocktail tables, talking in low voices. All the gaming tables were surrounded by clusters of gamblers. Chips were being handed back and forth across the green felt. The Zeta guys in their green visors looked smooth and professional, dealing out the cards and running the craps and roulette games like real croupiers. Bursts of laughter and smatterings of applause drifted up from the tables, mingling with the soft music.

Bess squeezed Paul's arm. "You've done an incredible job," she said lovingly.

"Hey, there's H. Samuel Porter," Paul said, nodding toward a distinguished-looking man with a drink in his hand leaning against a wall. "I want you to meet the guy responsible for bankrolling the whole weekend."

"Do I call him Sam or H. Sam or just H.?" Bess asked wryly as they approached.

Paul nuzzled her. *"You* call him *Mr.* Porter."

Bess held out her hand. "We're all really grateful, Mr. Porter," she said charmingly.

Porter gave Bess a fatherly smile. "It's my pleasure. I didn't make all my money to hoard it. These campus charities are first-rate organizations. And I must say, you kids have really put together a great night here. My son, who is quite a little card player already, is over there—"

Bess and Paul threw a glance toward the black-jack table.

"And he was speaking very highly of the dealer," Porter continued. "Everyone seems very well prepared and professional."

"Thank you, sir," Paul said, lowering his eyes modestly.

"And let me just add," Porter offered quietly, "that you two make a most handsome couple."

Bess blushed as Porter winked. She led Paul away, wrapping his arm around her waist. Up on stage Ray Johansson, the lead singer of the Beat Poets, was singing something sweet and slow, and Bess, her head against Paul's chest, started to sway her hips to the beat.

"Want to dance, Mr. Lucky?" she asked demurely.

"Only if I can dance with a certain beautiful blond woman," Paul replied.

"Here she is." Bess held him and closed her eyes. She could feel Paul's heartbeat against her ear. The night was just starting, but it was already a rousing success. There wasn't a doubt in her mind that this weekend was going to be wonderful.

"There's Nancy and Jake," Paul said, nodding toward the entrance.

Nancy was beaming. She looked sophisticated and stunning in a long sleeveless periwinkle blue dress with sparkling earrings and a matching choker. Her strawberry blond hair was swept off her face. Jake was dashing in his tux.

"You look so elegant!" Bess said as Nancy and Jake walked up.

Jake patted Paul's shoulder. "Everything's going great."

Nancy glanced appreciatively at Bess's dress. "Hmm," she said suspiciously. "And whose closet did we borrow this from?"

"We *bought* it—just today," Bess replied. "And you'll never guess who picked it out."

"George?"

"Try again. Think studious."

Nancy gasped. *"Leslie* went shopping with you."

"The very same," Bess replied.

"And now when I call," Paul interjected, "she actually asks if I'd like to leave a message."

Bess shook her head. "Just when life with Leslie was getting nice and predictable, she does an about-face, and goes and gets all friendly on me." Bess fanned herself dramatically. "All this excitement is making me thirsty," she said, offering her arm to Paul. "Sir, you may buy me a soda!"

Everything *is* okay, Paul thought to himself as he led Bess toward the drinks table in the back. But I just can't help being nervous.

The fact was, he'd never had so much responsibility in his life. Just having a beautiful girlfriend like Bess should be enough to calm his nerves. But Paul couldn't shake the fact that his fraternity had a bad reputation as a party house. All the other fraternities and sororities did lots of volunteer work, but Black & White Nights was the first really big benefit Zeta had ever been part of. There was a lot more than just making money riding on these two nights.

At the bar Paul asked for a couple of sodas and scanned the room as he waited for the drinks. Blackjack seemed to be the most popular game. The trustees and faculty were huddled around it three deep. A roar of laughter and applause drifted up, and Paul could see Billy, the dealer, shaking his head.

"Someone must be winning," he said, handing a glass to Bess.

"More than a little," Bess replied. "Nancy just said she overheard some guy saying that someone was cleaning up. He was on a ten-hand winning streak, or something like that."

Paul cocked his head. "Did you say *ten* hands?"

Bess shrugged. "That's what Nan said."

Paul remembered something he'd read in one of the gambling books he'd taken out of the library. Winning streaks in blackjack were supposed to be unusual. But *ten* games?

"I'll be right back," Paul whispered to Bess and snaked his way along the edge of the stage toward the blackjack table.

All he could see was the back of the guy's head. He was young, a college student, with fine, tawny hair. And most of the other players had dropped out. It was just this guy, a couple others, and the house playing one another.

Paul watched as the dealer carefully laid down the first cards, facedown, then the second, faceup. The guy immediately made a twenty-dollar bet, which was the limit they'd set on the table. He asked for a card, then another. The crowd hushed. Paul strained to see as everyone turned over their cards. The guy won again! The crowd applauded.

Paul squeezed his way to the front.

"This guy's too good to be true," he overheard an older man saying.

And he was. Paul watched as he won five consecutive hands, all for the twenty-dollar limit. He was betting as if he knew he couldn't lose. Paul counted the growing pile of chips in front of him and grimaced. He couldn't believe it.

"Six hundred dollars!" he muttered under his breath. "Lucky for him. But not so lucky for our charities!"

Bess was laughing hysterically. Just watching her friend made Nancy laugh herself. Jake was gesticulating wildly, going on and on about something. She'd missed what he'd said that was so funny. She thought it had something to do with Freddy. Jake might be a serious newspaper writer, but he was also a genius at telling wildly funny stories.

"I didn't know Jake was so funny, Nance," Bess said. "Doesn't he make you laugh all the time?"

Nancy smiled. "You get used to it."

Bess lifted her glass off the bar and raised it to her lips. But at the last second she pulled it away and peered inside.

"Jake!" she complained loudly.

"What did I do now?" he asked.

Lowering her glass out of view, Bess stuck her hand inside it.

"Bess, what are you doing!" Nancy laughed.

Bess fished around and pulled up something. She held it to the light, a small metal nugget, gold and black.

"That's my cuff link!" Jake said.

Bess laughed. "It *is*, and it was in my soda." She opened Jake's hand and pressed it into his palm.

"It's all sticky," Jake said.

Bess slapped Jake playfully. "I could have swallowed it!"

"Nah," Jake replied. He shook his head.

"Well, Freddy warned you those cuff links were old," Nancy reminded him. "But they were his last pair."

Jake shook his head. "I'm sure I'm going to end up paying for these." He turned to Nancy. "But it would be a small price to pay for such a great evening," he said affectionately.

"And such a handsome date," Nancy added, lifting her lips to be kissed.

"Uh-oh," Bess said, rolling her eyes. "An intimate moment. I'm out of here!"

"Yeah, go get your own intimate moment!" Nancy called after her with a laugh.

Seeing Jake fumbling with the cuff link, Nancy

pried his fingers away and put it on for him. "I don't want you wasting any of your attention on a pair of stupid cuff links," she said, "instead of on me. So if you do lose these, they're on me. Deal?"

Jake bent to whisper in her ear. "Let me think about it." He paused a beat. "Okay, I thought about it. It's a deal."

"In that case, let's go for a walk now," Nancy said.

Outside, there was a nip in the air, and Jake drew Nancy close. Through the windows, they could see Ray onstage, singing playfully to a table of older women.

"He's killing them," Jake said.

"Look at them," Nancy said thoughtfully. "They're falling in love."

Jake was peering at her, as if he wanted to ask something—or say something. She caressed Jake's chin, and drew it down to her level. Their bodies pressed together, and Nancy lost herself in a passionate kiss.

"I just can't believe how happy I am," she said between kisses. "It's not possible."

Jake grazed her lips with his. "You stole my line."

Nancy laughed softly. "You'd better watch out. That's what happens when you start spending too much time together—you start stealing each other's material. I can see it now"—Nancy waved her hand in front of their faces—"our new byline: Nancy Collins and Jake Drew."

"What have I stolen of yours?" Jake asked.

Nancy felt the corners of her mouth pull up. "My heart," she whispered. "You dirty thief."

CHAPTER 5

Breathing hard, Casey was nearing the end of the first set of her Vegas lounge act with Brian. Wearing a platinum blond wig and a bodysuit that she knew wouldn't leave much to anyone's imagination, she was doing her best to imitate Madonna, while Brian, in black leather from neck to toe, and a giant ankh pendant round his throat, was screeching his way through a routine by the artist formerly known as Prince.

The only way they could get away with it, Casey had always known, was if they hammed it up. The only problem was, being a ham was more exhausting than playing it straight.

Singing into her microphone and batting her eyelashes at a table of older gentlemen, Casey traced the path of a bead of sweat down the middle of her back. Her throat was dry. She needed a break.

I'm out of shape, she thought as she turned to Brian for the finale—a syrupy love duet.

She could hear the rhythmic applause starting already. She lifted her head, surprised, toward Nancy and Bess and the gang, who were standing in a row against the back wall, dancing and singing along. They were giving her a big thumbs-up and clapping over their heads. They looked hilarious, dressed up as if they were going to a ball but acting as if they were at a rock concert.

Casey felt an old familiar sensation—the surging nervous thrill whenever she performed, whether it was for television or the stage.

Out of the corner of her eye, she spotted Charley standing with his arms folded, his mouth upturned in a smile. He was loving it, too.

I bet he never thought I had Madonna in me, she thought just as her voice merged with Brian's in the final note.

Brian grabbed Casey's hand and together they stepped forward and swung into a low bow.

"Encore, encore!" people were shouting.

In the back her friends were applauding wildly.

"Good job, Case," Brian said as he followed her off. "For a second there, you even had me fooled."

Casey grinned wryly. "I guess there's a little

Madonna in all of us. And your Prince was out of sight! I loved the part when you fell on the stage and started writhing on your back."

"Yeah, but I don't think Porter approved." Brian laughed. "I saw him slap his forehead."

Casey leaned forward and whispered conspiratorially. "He loved it. All those old guys did. Can you imagine them break dancing?"

"You two had 'em in the palms of your hands," Charley said, sliding between them. He turned toward Casey. "Any room left in there for me?"

Casey grinned slyly. "You know there is. We have an hour until our next set. Is that enough time for you to crawl in?"

Charley winked at Brian. "See you later."

He took Casey's hand and headed for the exit.

"Where are we going?" she asked.

"I just wanted to talk," Charley began.

Casey glanced around the room. Onstage, the Beat Poets were tuning up their guitars for another set. People were everywhere, gambling, dancing, and talking. It was all so much fun and so exciting. "Can't we stay here?" she asked.

Charley glanced longingly at the door. "What's wrong with right outside, there in the dark—in real privacy?"

Casey sighed. "I've been working so hard, I just want to enjoy myself for a while. Come on, Charley, I only have an hour! Hey, Ginny—!"

she yelled as Ginny Yuen headed for the stage. "Get Ray to play something funky, and *fast!*"

Charley looked annoyed as she grabbed his hand and tugged him onto the dance floor. "I don't want to dance, Casey."

But Casey chose not to hear him and began to strut and writhe as the drummer of the Beat Poets started a quick rhythm on the cymbals. Charley didn't have any choice. Soon he and Casey were tearing up the dance floor. When the song pulled up short at the end, Casey and Charley finished their dance in an embrace.

"I'm so happy you came." Casey breathed in Charley's ear.

His expression turned serious. She knew he was still annoyed she wouldn't give him any private time.

Quickly Casey pressed a finger to his lips. "Not now," she panted, struggling to catch her breath. "I just want us to enjoy ourselves."

"They're amazing," Nancy said as Casey and Charley finished their dance with a formal whirl. "They make one of the greatest couples I've ever seen."

"Hey, you guys."

Nancy turned around. Paul was standing behind them with his hands in his pockets.

Nancy started rubbing his shoulders. "C'mon, Paul, remember how to have fun? That's F-U-N," she spelled. "Remember how to do that? Where's Bess? Now, *there's* a woman who knows how to have fun—"

Paul tilted his head. "She's over there. Somewhere."

Nancy stopped and inspected his face. "Ooh, I think it's serious. You'd better take two aspirin and call me in the morning."

"Are you still nervous?" Jake laughed.

"Unfortunately, now I think I have reason to be," Paul said, and told them about the guy cleaning up at the blackjack table.

"He's won how many hands in a row?" Jake inquired in disbelief.

"At this rate, he'll win a few thousand dollars by the end of the night," Paul explained.

"And you said he's a college student?" Nancy asked.

Paul just shook his head. "Maybe I didn't train my guys well enough."

Jake whistled. "I don't believe it."

Nancy headed across the room. "Me neither. I have to see this myself."

The audience around the blackjack table had more than doubled. Nancy recognized a few professors she'd seen around campus seated next to the guy Paul pointed out. When she squeezed through, Billy, the dealer, threw her a worried look and gestured with his head toward a young college-age kid. He was obviously very well-heeled: perfect posture, flawless light brown hair, and ice blue eyes.

The crowd fell silent as another hand was being dealt. Nancy noticed a couple of other students step up behind the kid who was winning. One of them patted him on the back. "Way to go, Sam. Keep it up."

"Thanks, Glenn," Sam said. "Do me a favor and get me a few of those little sweet-and-sour hors d'oeuvre things over there."

"Whatever," Glenn replied.

Sam squirmed in his seat as the second cards were being handed around. Nancy eyed the players. Everyone seemed edgy. Even Billy was shifting his feet, rubbing his hands. They all made their bets.

"The limit, as usual, Billy. Twenty bucks," Sam said. He nonchalantly chased away a stray hair with the flick of a finger. He hardly even blinked. And, of course, when they all turned over their cards, he'd won the hand. Murmurs spread through the crowd.

Sam didn't even smile. He just leaned forward, circled his hands around the pile of winnings, and added them to his huge mound of chips. "Maybe it's time to cash some of these in."

Billy looked suddenly relieved, until Sam laughed. "But I'm not going anywhere. It's just that all these chips are getting in my way!"

Glenn came back with a plate full of food and set it in front Sam.

Nancy snapped her fingers. "I've seen that guy—"

"Yeah, Freddy's," Jake threw in.

Nancy nodded. "That's him."

Jake looked at her. "So?"

Nancy shrugged. "Nothing, I guess. I mean, it's not like they're doing anything wrong, are they?"

"As far as I can see, that guy's cleaning up fair and square," Jake replied.

"That's what I'm afraid of," Paul said, coming up behind them. "But did you notice that every time he doesn't win, he always bets the minimum?"

"Yeah, and he has this annoying little laugh," Nancy added. "Like he meant to do it on purpose."

Jake said, "I hate guys like that."

Nancy glared at the back of Sam's head. "Me, too."

Daniel couldn't help noticing that despite the presence of dozens of beautiful women in revealing evening gowns, he was constantly pulled toward the very enticing face of Liz Bader. Liz was wearing something beautiful herself, a white chiffon dress. In fact, the way she was standing in front of the wheel of fortune, and the way she grinned under her phony platinum blond wig, made her a dead ringer for a famous game-show hostess.

Liz smiled suggestively. "Would you like a spin?"

"I wouldn't mind trying my luck." Daniel laughed. "This was a terrific last-minute idea to have you dress up like that game-show hostess. You look great."

Liz sidled up to him, her mouth set in a playful smile. "Are you going to make your donation? Nothing's free, you know."

Daniel met her stare and took out his wallet.

"Five dollars a spin," Liz said.

"Five!" Daniel exclaimed. "But it says two—"

Liz leaned forward and plucked a five-dollar bill out of his wallet. "It's usually two. But you"—she wagged a finger and narrowed her eyes—"I have a feeling about you. You're about to find your pot of gold. Better make it five."

Daniel nodded. "Whatever you say."

Liz gave the wheel a hard spin. The dollar awards and other prizes reeled by in blurred splashes of rainbow colors. But Daniel kept his eye on the Day-Glo *Jackpot!* that Liz had painted. That's what he wanted.

The wheel was slowing. Liz was peering up at it, just as hard as Daniel was. There it was, the *Jackpot!,* slowing near the top!

"Ooh," Liz said, excitedly clapping her hands.

She leaned forward as it came round. "Oh . . . oh, no, no, wait . . . stop!"

Daniel stared at his prize: *Bankrupt!*

He chuckled good-naturedly, but inwardly he wondered whether it was a sign.

Liz suddenly perked up. "Don't worry. It's just a game."

"It is?"

"Yup," Liz said with that slick TV poise. She was the TV hostess again. "I'm sure you'll get your wish anyway."

Daniel smiled. "But how do you know what it is?"

Liz tapped her temple. "I've spun this wheel for enough people tonight. I can read their faces. I know what you wished for."

Daniel stared at her. "And?"

Liz shrugged and threw up her hands. "Who knows? I guess you'll just have to wait and see."

"I thought it was a sign," Daniel said, not wanting to go, but seeing that his time was up. Other people were waiting for a spin.

Liz stared hard at him. "It *is* a sign."

"But it said 'Bankrupt.' "

Liz walked forward in three determined strides. Daniel stepped back, surprised.

She pressed a finger into his chest. "If I were you, mister, I wouldn't believe everything you read." And she kissed him gently on the lips.

*   *   *

Bess felt like the star of her own little movie. Even though Casey was a real star, Bess was the date of the night's big star. Besides, Bess had been in on all of the preparations, too, so why shouldn't she bask in some of the glory?

And she was—until now.

Paul, the man of her dreams, had gone from nervous to sad, from sad to worried, and now, from worried to depressed.

"He can't stop obsessing over it," she said as she, Nancy, George, Will, Holly, and Eileen watched Sam roll over everyone at the blackjack table. Paul was standing behind a new dealer, watching Sam's every move. He'd relieved Billy over an hour ago, but Sam kept on rolling.

"It's too good to be true," Holly said, her voice filled with wonder.

"And Paul can't do anything about it," Nancy said.

"It's not like he's cheating," Bess suggested.

"Not in the open, anyway" was Nancy's quick reply. "He could be lucky, but he just acts too sure of himself. I don't like it, either."

"Has Paul changed decks?" Eileen wondered.

Bess nodded. "When he changed the dealer. It's like Sam has ESP or something."

"Or he knows what the cards are even before they're played," George added.

A few people stepped back and made a path as H. Samuel Porter waded toward the table.

"Coming to play, Mr. Porter?" Bess asked, relieved that maybe *he* could find a way to beat Sam.

Mr. Porter put a friendly hand on Bess's shoulder. "No, dear. I'm just coming by to say hello."

"Well, you couldn't have picked a more interesting table," Nancy commented.

"Oh, and why is that?"

Bess nodded toward Sam. "Just watch."

Ten minutes later four more hands had been played and won by the unflinching Sam.

Porter stepped forward, and, to Bess's dismay, tapped Sam on the shoulder. "On a winning streak?"

Sam looked up nervously, then smiled. "Just lucky, Dad," he said with a shrug.

Porter patted him on the back. "Well, have fun, but don't forget what tonight is really for. Leave some for the charities."

Bess swallowed. She, Nancy, and George exchanged horrified looks. Porter was Sam's father!

Porter took a step toward Paul, his disapproval and uneasiness written all over his face. "Setting a winner's limit would have been the *smart* thing to do," he said peevishly. "This is supposed to be a fund-raiser, you know."

As Porter sauntered away, Bess could see that Paul was upset. She grabbed Paul's hand. "You okay?"

Paul shook his head. Bess could feel the frustration coursing through him. "Porter's right," he said. "But I never thought we'd need a winner's limit."

"It's not your fault, you know," Bess said quickly.

"It *is* our fault if Sam's not winning fairly," Nancy interjected.

Paul eyed her. "What are you saying?"

"I'll tell you what I'd say," Jake proposed, stepping in. "I've seen people gamble before. What's going on here seems just too good to be true. I don't think any guy could win so much so quickly, unless he knows what cards are coming next."

Bess noticed Nancy listening carefully.

"But he's Porter's son," Bess said.

Nancy shook her head. "Which makes it a very sticky situation."

"Yeah," Paul said, almost laughing at the irony. "Porter's not only bankrolling this whole event, he's also the wealthiest member of the Wilder board. And the most powerful. We can't exactly ask his son to stop playing now, can we?"

We've all worked so hard, Bess thought, disheartened, but no one as hard as Paul.

"Well, at least we know how Sam got in here tonight," Nancy said, staring off into the distance, "since he's not part of the Black and White Nights Organization Committee, and couldn't have gotten in free. Porter must have paid for his ticket.

That's five hundred bucks. Not a small amount for a college kid. And Sam's two friends—"

"Must have wealthy alumni parents, too," Bess finished the thought.

Everyone seemed to let out a collective sigh at the thought.

"Which leaves us where?" Nancy asked rhetorically.

Bess grimaced. "Absolutely nowhere."

CHAPTER 6

Daniel leaned back in his chair, taking a break from the party cleanup. The rest of the crew was picking up and getting everything set for the next night, when it would be twice as crowded, this time with students. The last of the partygoers had left, and the Beat Poets were putting away their instruments. Daniel sneaked a peek at Liz far across the big room. She'd changed out of her glittering white dress into sweats and a T-shirt.

"Earth to Frederick," a deep voice said behind him.

Daniel snapped around.

"Didn't you hear me calling you?" Paul asked.

Daniel shook his head. "I was off in my own world."

Paul followed Daniel's gaze across the room toward Liz. "She won't be done cleaning up for a while. Can you give me a hand?"

Daniel pushed himself up. "Where are you taking me, 'O Captain! my Captain!'" he wisecracked.

"Downstairs—with this," Paul answered, showing Daniel a gray metal box.

Daniel raised an eyebrow, then nodded.

"Come on," Paul said. "There's a lot of cash in here. Though not a quarter of what's already downstairs. I've been taking money down all night."

"Aren't you lucky," Daniel quipped.

Paul grimaced. "Don't joke. There's a lot less money than there could be, thanks to our friendly neighborhood cardsharp."

Daniel eyed the box. He wondered why Paul hadn't hired a security guard or anything.

"Is all that cash safe?" he asked skeptically.

Paul winked. "I have a system. Let's go."

Daniel followed Paul down into the basement and through the maze of hallways.

Paul finally ducked into a tiny office at the end of a hall. "The storeroom with the supplies is a few doors down. This is our bank."

Inside, he squatted down next to a small black safe and punched in some numbers on a computer lock set in the door. The lock clicked, and Paul opened the door. Paul took out a metal strongbox, and using a key on his key ring, unlocked it. From inside, he pulled up a pile of cash and checks. He counted the cash while Daniel tallied the checks.

"We have . . . wow . . . twenty-five thousand in checks!" Daniel breathed.

Paul waved a stack of bills. "And I have fifteen thousand in cash."

Daniel whistled, amazed. He'd never seen that much money in one place in his life.

They both looked at it in silence.

"That's a lot of dough," Daniel said.

"You're not kidding," Paul said worriedly. He put the money back in the strongbox, and it snapped shut. Sliding it into the safe, Paul closed the door and the lock clicked closed.

"Say, why don't you tell me the computer code for the lock," Daniel joked. "Just in case you forget it," he added.

"Yeah, right," Paul replied. "Thanks but no thanks. Only Mr. Porter and I have the code."

Daniel raised his eyebrows in a questioning manner.

"This is Mr. Porter's donation," Paul explained. "He bought it for us to use for the weekend."

Daniel peered at it. "Really? So Porter got it for you, huh? Nice of him. Who gets it afterward?"

"It goes back to Porter's." Paul shrugged.

"He'll probably use it as a personal office safe at his house."

Daniel chuckled. "Well, since you have the computer code for the lock, doesn't that make his safe a little vulnerable? Not that you'd try to rip him off, off course."

"Ha, ha, very funny. As a matter of fact, the code can be reset. So Porter can make a new code for the lock." Paul narrowed his eyes and stared at Daniel.

"And don't think of trying to cart it off, either," he said jokingly. "It must weigh about eighty to one hundred pounds, all hard steel, double-thick. It took two heavy-duty moving guys to get it in here."

Daniel held up his hands. "Whatever you say," he said. "I'm heading back upstairs. I told Liz I'd help her clean up."

"Yeah, I noticed you working hard when I saw you," Paul deadpanned. "Go on up. I have some organizing to do down here. Oh, when you see Bess, let her know I'm ready to go to the bank any time. I'll wait for her in the supply room. I just want to check our inventory for tomorrow night."

Daniel looked at his watch and cocked his head. "It's almost two in the morning. Don't banks close in the afternoon?"

Paul shook his head. "Night deposit. At the Credit Union. Those little metal doors on the outside of banks about the size of a loaf of bread? They're for storekeepers, so they can get their money into the bank, where it's a lot safer than if it's left at their stores overnight."

"And the Credit Union is letting you use theirs?"

Paul dangled his key ring and shook it. "We opened an account last week."

Daniel nodded with admiration. "I have to admit, you have everything covered."

Paul shook his head sadly. "I wish."

Daniel looked at him. "That cardsharp? I'm sorry I missed seeing that guy play tonight. Hey, don't let him get to you. Black and White Nights made a ton of money today. And there's still another day to go."

Paul nodded slowly, seeing the light.

"Feel better?" Daniel said. "Good, because I'm beat. I'm out of here!"

By the time Daniel made his first wrong turn in the hallways, he realized he should have asked Paul for directions. But it was too late. He was lost, although he thought he knew where he was going.

"Or sort of knew," Daniel muttered to himself, looking right and left down a hallway.

Finally Daniel saw an Exit sign near a stairway, and he made a beeline for it. But just as he turned, he ran into a couple of guys in tuxedos.

One of them had a long flip of black hair over his eyes.

"We're looking for the bathroom," one of them said quickly.

Daniel laughed. "You're kidding, right?"

The other guy, with the black hair, shook his head. "No, really. Someone pointed us down here."

"Well, whoever did, don't talk to them again," Daniel joked. "They're not your friends."

The hair guy grimaced. "You mean it's not down here?"

Daniel shook his head. "It's no wonder you got lost. But here's a tip: There are bathrooms *above* ground."

"Thanks," they said, and trailed Daniel tiredly up the stairs.

"Wow, my legs are tired," Daniel complained as he struggled up.

"Yeah, us, too."

"You guys do okay?" Daniel asked, continuing the march up.

The two men exchanged amused looks. The guy with the black hair shrugged. "We did okay. You know what they say. You win some and you lose some. But it was a great party."

Suddenly Daniel turned. "But you two do know the party's over, don't you?"

"Hey, the party's *never* over, dude!" the other man said with a snicker.

*   *   *

Bess leaned in the doorway of the downstairs supply room for Black & White Nights, watching Paul stalk up and down past the boxes, checking to make sure they had enough of everything for the next night.

"Cups . . . plates," he muttered. "Soda . . ."

I never knew he talked to himself, she thought, amused. Right now he could write the book on adorable!

Paul had taken off his tuxedo jacket and bow tie and undid a few of his top shirt buttons. There was only the cummerbund left, which Bess thought was kind of sexy. Happily watching Paul rake his fingers through his hair, she thought he looked gorgeous.

Finally she spoke, "Hi, sexy."

When Paul's eyes met Bess's, a weary smile spread across his face. He took a step toward her and without saying a word gave her a big hug. "Boy, have I missed you," he said. "Where have you been?"

"Giving Nancy, George, and Holly a hand upstairs," Bess replied. "Daniel said you were waiting for me."

"How long have you been standing there?"

Bess shrugged innocently. "Oh, I don't know. Not long enough. I could watch you all night."

Paul turned and picked up a notebook where he'd scrawled some numbers. "Look how much we made tonight. Almost forty thousand dollars! Even *with* Mr. Smooth at the blackjack table."

Bess gave a little relieved laugh and took Paul's hand in hers. "See? Didn't I say everything would work out? I told you not to worry so much."

Paul led Bess out of the storeroom and down the hall to the office. Inside, he threw a glimpse toward the safe. "I'll worry a lot less once we get the money in night deposit. I'm almost ready to go. Now, where did that bank bag go?"

Bess put a free arm around Paul's waist. Then the other arm. She craned her neck and planted a kiss under his chin.

Suddenly she was in Paul's arms and being kissed breathless.

"Wow!" she said airily. "Where'd *that* come from? I thought you were about to crash on me."

Paul nuzzled her ear and smiled. "I was."

"Maybe the night deposit can wait?" Bess asked suggestively.

"What do you mean? I have to get the money over there."

"Come on," Bess said softly. "Forget the money for a minute. It's in a locked safe. Look at *me*. Think about *me*." She kissed him hard on the lips.

Paul felt himself filling with pleasure as the tension and weariness of the day melted away in Bess's long and sweet kiss. Why not, he thought as his mind slid more and more into their passionate embrace. No one can get into that safe. It'll be okay until tomorrow. He kissed her harder.

When they finally broke for air, Bess said breathlessly, "That's what I've been waiting for all night." She tightened her grip around his neck.

Paul looked into her beautiful face, drinking in her soft blue eyes and warm rosy lips. "Right now, all I want is to be with you," he said huskily. "We're out of here."

Nancy slowly sat down outside, at the side of Hewlitt's wide, stone steps, in the shadow of a streetlight. Groaning, she pulled off her pumps and wriggled her toes. "Well, they're still all there," she said to herself. She rubbed her feet. "I'll get Ginny to tell the Poets not to be so good tomorrow night."

Nancy chuckled to herself as she remembered Casey and Brian's lounge act.

Brian is such a natural ham, she thought, picturing him falling to his knees and screeching into the microphone. Most of the trustees and faculty had just stared at him, completely aghast, because they didn't know who he was pretending to be.

Just then Nancy heard voices. "So what did I tell you, was I right or was I right?" one voice asked.

Nancy twisted around. Three guys in tuxedos were walking down the steps. She squinted in the dark and recognized Sam and his friends, Glenn and Jack. She leaned farther back into the shadows and listened.

"You were right, Sam," one of them said.

Sam laughed. "Jack, if you think I was right tonight, just wait until tomorrow night—"

Tomorrow night? she repeated to herself. Great. Paul's really going to love that.

Someone else pushed through the doors behind the three guys, and they fell silent. Then Sam spoke up, quickly changing the subject. "How about a sub at the Hot Truck?"

They disappeared down the path.

"Nancy?"

It was Jake, standing in the middle of the steps, peering into the dark. Nancy wearily got to her feet and silently sneaked up behind him in her stocking feet.

"Right here," she whispered in his ear.

"Can we go home now?" Jake asked after he got over being startled.

"One more dance," Nancy joked.

Jake groaned. Nancy leaned on him. "Okay, okay. Though I wouldn't exactly call Thayer Hall home." She started walking. Jake caught up and, taking her elbow, led her toward the quad.

The grass was cold, wet, and springy under Nancy's feet. "Oh, the grass feels great!"

They crossed the grassy quad toward Thayer Hall. Except for the occasional footsteps of someone walking home from a frat party or a concert, the night was silent.

"I don't really want the evening to end yet," Jake said.

Nancy laughed. "That's just what I was thinking. But Kara's probably upstairs. I wouldn't want to wake her."

"Let's go back to my place," Jake offered. "We can hang out together for a while and talk."

Nancy flashed a wry smile. "And maybe do more than just talk?"

Jake shrugged. "Well, that's up to you, Ms. Drew. I, for one, am tired of talking."

Nancy raised herself on her tiptoes and whispered in Jake's ear, "Good."

Jake slung his jacket over his shoulder. They crossed the streets toward Jake's off-campus apartment in an old Victorian house.

"Walking without shoes feels so terrific!" Nancy laughed, and gripped Jake's hand harder. Her heart was galloping. Stealing a quick glance at Jake, she wondered if he was feeling as happy as she was.

"Home," Jake said softly when they reached his door. "Sort of."

Nancy reached up and kissed him softly.

But when Jake opened the door, there was anything but the privacy Nancy and he had been anticipating. Nick Dimartini and Dennis Larkin, Jake's roommates, were draped over the couch watching TV. Empty pizza boxes, soda cans, and ice cream pints lay strewn over the floor.

"Had a party tonight?" Jake wondered.

"No, just us," Nick replied blithely.

Jake snorted. "A little hungry, maybe? Hey, haven't you seen that movie fifty times already?"

But Nick's and Dennis's eyes were glued to the screen, as if in a trance. Their faces were blue in the TV light. "Sixty," Nick replied drolly.

Nancy sighed. Why couldn't we be alone? she lamented inwardly.

"You guys are slobs." Jake laughed, and led Nancy back out into the hall. "Sorry," he said.

Nancy smiled. "Don't worry. I'm still crazy about you."

"Maybe tomorrow night we can have the place to ourselves," Jake said hopefully.

They walked out onto the wide wraparound front porch of the house and sat on the old love seat.

"Sounds great." They sat quietly, arms wrapped around each other, both lost in thought.

Nancy sat up after a minute and looked at Jake.

"Just before you came out of the Hewlitt, I overheard Sam talking to his two friends," Nancy said.

"Blackjack Sam?" Jake asked.

Nancy nodded. "He said something about how Saturday night is going to be even better than tonight was."

Jake whistled. "Well, if he plays as well tomorrow as he did tonight, you can kiss a lot more of that fund-raiser money goodbye."

"Or if he cheats as well," Nancy said aloud.

Jake shook his head. "But how could he have cheated? He had a crowd around him all night."

"No one could be that good—or that lucky. We should talk to Paul about setting up a winning limit for tomorrow night," she suggested. "Once you hit it, you're done."

Jake shrugged. "I don't know if that's a great idea. One, we're not totally positive Sam cheated, as much as we'd like to think he did. Two, it wouldn't be fair to everyone else. Why punish the rest of the student body because of one annoying guy?"

"Because he'll clean us out," Nancy replied.

But she knew Jake was right. However, she for one didn't want to stand around again, watching Sam vacuum up all those chips.

"We could all take shifts keeping a close eye on him," she pondered. "What do you think? Maybe we can figure out his secret?"

Jake took Nancy in his arms. "I think you can figure out anything you want."

CHAPTER 7

I don't know *why* you had to get me up so early," Stephanie drawled, listlessly fingering through the racks at Selena's.

Kara laughed, and Stephanie found her just too perky. Kara, in fact, was just too *everything* right now.

"It's noon, Steph," Kara said. "Most people have been up for hours. I have to find something for tonight. Hey, what about this?"

Kara held a red baby-doll with a yellow and black flowered print up to her neck.

Wincing, Stephanie shielded her eyes. "There's a reason it's marked Sale."

Kara stared at it. "Why, what's wrong with it?"

Stephanie clucked her tongue. "What season are we currently experiencing?"

"Fall." Kara at first looked perplexed, and then as if a light bulb had gone off in her head she added, "Oh, not *summer*." She seemed momentarily dejected, but returning to her own buoyant self, she moved, humming, to the next rack.

Boy, am I dying for a cigarette, Stephanie thought to herself. She looked longingly toward the door, which was wide open, letting in a cool, gentle breeze. "Later," she muttered to herself.

Stephanie focused on the clothes. Now for me, she thought, I'm in the mood for something that's nothing short of devastating. It has to do double duty: I want to look ravishing tonight, and whatever I buy has to cost a fortune.

Holding up a beautiful, bright yellow silk dress, Stephanie scowled. "This dress is horrid!"

"No, it's not. It's sweet!" Kara exclaimed, running to rescue it from Stephanie's grip.

"Exactly," Stephanie shot back, flipping back a piece of her black hair. "Who wants sweet?"

Not my father, Stephanie thought, a picture of her stepmother coming into her mind. *Sweet* was the very last word on Stephanie's mind when it came to her father's new twenty-eight-year-old wife, Kiki. Stephanie hadn't met her yet, but she hated her already.

Her finger stopped on something black, silk, sheer, and unimaginably tight.

"There you are," she murmured softly, sliding

the dress off its hangar. "What's a nice tarty dress like you doing in a dull, dreary store like this?"

"Wow, that dress is a man-eater, and it costs huge bucks!" Kara said, peeking over Stephanie's shoulder at the price tag.

Stephanie brandished her father's credit card like a weapon. Her eyes flashing, her pouty, bloodred lips narrowed into a triumphant grin. "Precisely."

Kara offered her a purple silk scarf. "How about this, too?"

Stephanie smiled. "All the better to tie Daddy and Stepmommy in knots with—especially when they get the bill!"

Casey's mind was racing a mile a minute. She was standing before her mirror, trying to take advantage of the peace and quiet in the room without Stephanie. She not-so-casually dropped the suggestion to Kara to take Stephanie shopping, then had to sweeten the deal by offering to lend her a pair of her favorite earrings. Anything to be able to concentrate on her work.

"Okay," she told herself. "From one o'clock to three o'clock Russian lit paper; from three o'clock to four o'clock, read; from four o'clock to six o'clock, get ready for tonight. Wait, wait," She knew she was leaving something out. "Okay, from four o'clock to four-oh-five o'clock, talk to Charley."

Casey pursed her lips. "Sorry, Charley," she said under her breath. "But you should have called first." Just then she was startled by a knock on her door.

"Casey?" It was Charley's voice coming through the door. And he didn't sound very happy.

Casey glanced at her watch. She was behind schedule. Taking a deep breath, she flung open the door.

"Hi," Charley said, not a trace of happiness on his face.

"Um, how was the motel?" she asked sheepishly.

"Lonely," he replied dryly.

Casey kissed him lightly on the lips. "I'm really sorry. But I wasn't lying when I said I wasn't feeling great."

"I can't believe I came all this way to sleep on a lumpy bed at the Collegetown Motel—*alone.*"

Casey sighed. "I was exhausted. I *really* needed the sleep." She gestured behind her at her cluttered desk. "And all this work I had to get done on top of it."

Charley looked inconsolable. "The bed was lousy. I feel all stiff."

Casey smiled warmly. "You look pretty tight. Want to come in? But only for a sec. I've got to—"

"Casey, this is the first time I've had you alone

in twenty-four hours," Charley interrupted. He shut the door and backed up against it.

Casey sighed and lowered herself onto the edge of her bed. After all, Charley *did* come all this way.

"Okay," she said. "I know you've been wanting to talk to me. So now I'm listening. I'm all ears."

Charley was gazing at her, his eyes full of love. Casey had to smile. He was so gorgeous and sweet. She stood up and held his hand. "What is it?"

Charley smiled, embarrassed. "I can't believe I'm about to say what I'm about to say," he began.

Just then the door was pushed open against Charley's back.

"Ow!" he cried, grabbing his shoulder.

"Hey, let me in!"

Casey closed her eyes. "Oh, no!"

Charley stepped aside, and Stephanie barged in, dragging Kara.

"Kara, I told you *two* hours," Casey mouthed.

Kara opened her mouth in a silent scream. She didn't have to explain. Casey knew what it could be like to spend a lot of time with Stephanie, especially if she was in a foul mood.

Casey cringed as Stephanie started to get angry. "I can't believe I was barred from my very own dorm room! Oh, it's you," she said, suddenly demure when she noticed Charley.

Casey saw that Charley was staring at Stephanie in dismay. But obviously Stephanie didn't care. She perked right up, smiling innocently. None of her wicked witch routine in front of a handsome man! Casey thought.

"Why, I just bought a new dress," Stephanie said directly to Charley. "It's modest but practical. Would you like me to model it for you? I mean, *you*," she added, tossing a look at Casey as an afterthought.

"Maybe later?" Casey said delicately.

She noticed Charley's right eyebrow twitching. It only did that when he was frustrated and mad. Casey had witnessed it a handful of times, mostly on the set of *The President's Daughter*, when their director was driving him crazy.

But he can take care of himself, Casey reminded herself. You have a schedule to keep.

"Sorry to break up the party, guys," Casey broke in. "But I've got to go to the library. I have a paper due on Monday—"

"Library?" Charley cried.

"You want to come?" Casey asked, with no real enthusiasm.

Charley stared at her and sighed.

"You can hang out with me," Stephanie suggested, sidling up to Charley. "I *never* go to the library. Here. Feel." Stephanie held up the hem of her new dress and rubbed it against Charley's face.

Charley looked as if he wanted to explode with frustration. Casey swallowed a laugh.

"Cheer up," she said. "In a couple of hours we'll be going to another party. We'll have a blast tonight, I promise."

The hallway of Suite 301 was crammed with women in various stages of undress. Everyone was twisting around to get in and out of rooms. Tying back her strawberry blond hair in a scrunchie, Nancy lowered her shoulder and plunged into the crush.

But her room wasn't any better. Kara, Bess, and Eileen were playfully elbowing one another, vying for a clear piece of the mirror. Kara was standing in a fluffy bath sheet, Bess had on a funky red dress that set off her golden hair, and Eileen was wearing something blue and tight. Makeup and hair accessories were scattered around the room.

"Tonight's not black tie, you know," Nancy reminded them.

Bess frowned. "Yeah, but how often do we get the chance to dress up in gorgeous clothes?"

"Sexy clothes, is more like it," Eileen commented it.

Nancy sighed. "I guess I'll just have to wear my black Lycra micro-mini."

"Perfect!" Bess cried.

Reva poked her head in the room. "Males have breached the walls!" she warned with mock alarm.

"Whose?" Bess asked.

"Yours," she replied.

Bess quickly put on her lipstick. "Is he wearing his sexy cummerbund? If he's not wearing his cummerbund, tell him I'm not coming out."

The women broke into laughter as Reva stuck her head back out into the hall. She gave a thumbs-up. "Cummerbund—check," she said with a wink.

"I'm out of here!" Bess said, racing away.

"See you later!" Nancy called after her.

Bess collided with Liz in the doorway, and both quickly sprinted back to mirrors to assess their damage. After a few seconds of primping, Bess winked at her own reflection and was gone.

"Tim and Daniel are here, Kara," Liz said.

"What's up with you and Daniel, anyway?" Nancy wanted to know.

Liz smiled softly and shrugged. "We've talked about what happened. I think things are going to be okay."

"Well, you two do seem made for each other," Nancy commented. "He couldn't keep his eyes off you all night. It was like no one else was in the room."

Kara ran by, dropping her handbag in Liz's arms while she glanced over her shoulder to get a last glimpse of her new dress from the back.

"Well, I think you two are so paralyzed by love that you can't eat, sleep, talk on the phone, study, or have any fun at all until you just break down and admit it to each other."

Nancy nodded. "I guess she has it all figured out," she deadpanned.

Kara shrugged friskily. "It's only my opinion. Let's go, lovebird," she said, and pulled Liz out of the room.

Without warning Jake appeared in the doorway, wearing an appreciative grin on his face.

"The most beautiful woman on campus," Jake said admiringly.

Nancy shifted her eyes in his direction. "You're not too bad yourself."

Nancy and Jake gazed at each other. She didn't need to hear him say a thing. It was all in his beautiful piercing brown eyes.

"I miss you more now than I did five minutes ago," she whispered as she wrapped him in an embrace.

"But here I am," Jake replied.

Nancy shrugged. "I know," she said. She rested her head against his chest, and listened to his heartbeat, shutting out the outside noise.

After a minute Jake released her. "Ready?"

Nancy brushed on one last dab of blush. Her sky blue eyes glittered. "I'm ready," she echoed on a breathy note.

*   *   *

Halfway across the quad, Jake could tell that this night's Casino night was going to be nothing like the one the night before. The place was already rocking! The Beat Poets had turned up the volume, filling the night air with strains of electric guitar and drumbeats. The lively crowd was already overflowing onto the lawn. A lot of them weren't bothering to wait to get inside to start dancing.

"Now, this is more like it," Jake said.

Nancy squeezed his hand excitedly.

Inside, there was even more of a carnival atmosphere. Every table was crowded.

But Jake was most interested in one blackjack table. The one Sam was sitting at—again. And, to Jake's dismay, just like last night, the audience at that particular table was bigger than at any other table. Occasionally the crowd around it applauded, as if they were at a tennis match.

"That's not a good sign," Jake muttered, giving Nancy's hand a squeeze before heading over to it. He snaked his way to the front. But before he got there, he spotted the back of Sam's head. He was sitting in the same seat, and Jake wasn't surprised when he saw that his pile of chips was already much bigger than anyone else's.

He caught Paul's eye across the table. Paul looked upset, and Jake noticed Daniel and Holly, standing near the dealer, observing Sam's every move.

"This time we've got him covered," Jake whispered to Nancy as she came up to join him. "If he is cheating, we're going to catch him."

They both watched in silence as Sam easily won two more hands.

"Well, I guess there's nothing left to do now but have some fun?" Nancy said, turning away Jake moved with her into the crowd.

"Wait, what's that?" Jake heard someone call out.

Jake and Nancy turned their heads toward the stage. Ray came on wearing a white bodysuit, long sideburns, and tinted glasses. In a low, crooning voice he started to sing.

"It's Elvis!" Nancy laughed, grabbing Jake's hand.

Jake bent down and whispered in Nancy's ear. "I bet you didn't know that I crumble when I hear the king of rock 'n' roll. I'll do *anything!*"

Nancy batted her eyes in an exaggerated way. "Do you have Elvis back at your place?" she asked suggestively.

Even though Nancy was obviously kidding around, Jake couldn't deny the twinge of anticipation he was feeling. If he could have, he would have swept Nancy into his arms and taken her away right then.

CHAPTER 8

As Reva and Andy were getting something cold to drink, she was thinking about clothes. Which wasn't that surprising. Reva and everyone else in her suite had been thinking about nothing but clothes for an entire week. They obsessed about what to wear on Saturday night and what everyone *else* was wearing on Saturday night.

In fact, Reva had never seen the Wilder student body looking so good. Kids she recognized from classes were totally transformed: no more sweats, T-shirts, and jeans. Tonight Hewlitt was filled with chenille and silk and fancy dress shirts. There were bow ties shaped like fish and dresses that glittered like gold.

Reva knew her outfit was hot. After a lot of

deliberation, she had decided to go simple and classy: flowing white pants and a silvery silk top with black strap high heels. With her deeply burnished skin, and her high cheekbones, she knew she looked just right.

And that's just how I feel, she thought, gazing adoringly at Andy, whose raven black eyes and black hair were set off handsomely by his black tux.

Admit it, Reva thought to herself: He's a stud.

Suddenly Reva felt her shoulder being tapped. She turned around.

"Hi, Reva!" an all-too-familiar guy said.

"Darrell?"

Darrell smiled. "Having fun?" he asked.

Out of the corner of her eye, Reva could see Andy observing them.

"Sure," Reva answered. Darrell was a computer technician who had fixed some glitches in her computer a couple of times. Andy knew more about computer software than anyone she knew, but he couldn't fix delicate problems inside the hard drive, which was where the glitch was. So he told her to call Campus Computer, and tall, dark, handsome Darrell came knocking on her door with his bag of tools. He was good-looking and sweet, but he had asked Reva out twice, even though she'd told him she had a boyfriend.

"Want to dance?" Darrell asked, taking her hand.

Reva smiled stiffly. Andy folded his arms, an

amused grin on his face as he looked from Reva to Darrell and back again, waiting to be introduced.

"Just a short one," Darrell said, "Come on."

"This is Andy Rodriguez," Reva quickly introduced him, pulling her hand free, "my boyfriend."

"Darrell Jones," he replied, shaking Andy's hand. "You're an incredibly lucky guy."

Andy nodded. "Thanks."

"Mind if Reva and I have a dance?"

Reva looked nervously at Andy, but he seemed to find this whole thing very amusing.

"No, Reva doesn't need my permission," Andy replied.

Darrell grabbed Reva's hand and tugged her into the middle of the dance floor. "Thanks," he called as they passed Andy. "I'll have her back in a minute."

Reva threw Andy an I-can't-help-it look, but he'd turned away before he saw her.

Darrell wasn't a bad dancer. And the song was great. But Reva would much rather have been in Andy's arms. She danced as if she had cement in her arms and legs, barely moving.

When the song ended, she wriggled her fingers in a lukewarm wave. "Thanks, Darrell. That was fun. But I have to get back to my date now."

She spun around and left Darrell behind.

"Andy!" she cried, and slalomed through the

crowd. She grabbed the tail of his jacket and tugged. "I'm sorry," she said. "I had no idea."

"So that's the computer guy, huh?" Andy asked, a mischievous glint in his eye. "Those guys get better looking every day.

"Yes." Reva nodded. "He was just over yesterday to fix something on my computer. I'm really sorry—"

"Well, he likes you," Andy teased, poking her in the side. "That's obvious."

Reva didn't deny it. It was true, Darrell really seemed to have a thing for her. She shrugged. "Who cares? I'm here with you, and this particular song happens to be a favorite of mine, and we're wasting it standing here—"

"Hey, you guys!" It was Nancy, dancing by with Jake. Or was that Jake dancing by with Nancy? Reva couldn't tell. But it made her smile. They were a great couple, totally at ease with each other, and having fun dancing uninhibitedly. Even though Jake wasn't the greatest dancer in the world

"Come on," Reva beseeched Andy, giving his finger a little tug. "Darrell is nice. But *this* man"—Reva wrapped her hands around Andy's waist—"is currently the answer to my dreams."

"Really?" Andy asked.

Reva nodded resolutely. "Really."

They started dancing again, but Reva slipped and stumbled on something. A glint of metal flashed on the floor. She reached down and picked up a cuff link.

Jake danced over, moaning. "Thanks," he said, plucking the cuff link out of Reva's hand. He held it up to the light, like a scientific specimen. "I'm definitely going to lose this thing." He danced away.

"But I hope you'll never lose this," Andy said to Reva.

She glanced down. He'd slipped a slim white box into her hand. "Andy, what . . ." she started to ask.

Staring down at the box, excitement ran through her. Andy had never given her a gift before.

She looked up and held Andy's loving gaze with her own.

"Open it," he said.

Reva slipped off the cover and sucked in her breath. It was a delicate gold bracelet, with a lovely gold heart charm with a cluster of pearls in the center. As Reva held it up to the light, she glimpsed something on the other side of the heart. "What's on it?"

Andy was smiling.

"My initial!" she cried. The charm had a beautiful *R* engraved in the middle, in a flowery script.

"I can't believe you!" Reva cried happily, circling her arms around Andy's neck.

"We're not just partners in our business," he said softly into her ear, "we're partners in love, too."

Reva was beaming. "Partners in love."

"Alone again," Bess moaned, dramatically touching the back of her hand to her forehead.

Nodding with shared grief, Brian Daglian put his arm around her, patting her shoulder.

"It must be hard being the girlfriend of such a responsible man," Brian quipped as they watched Paul circling the gambling tables, making sure everything was running smoothly.

"What's hard is checking on what everyone's eating," Bess replied with a shrug. "Hmm, barbecued spare ribs. Cold sesame noodles . . ."

Her stomach gave a plaintive rumble, and she led Brian across the dance floor toward the caterers' tables. Halfway there she abruptly stopped and Brian crashed into her.

"I can't believe it!" Bess said.

Leslie, in a prim but classy blue dress, was putting together a plate of food. Bumping elbows with a very tall guy next to her, she actually laughed and apologized. Was that really a glitter in her eyes?

"I wish I had my camera," Bess said with wonder.

Brian shook his head in amazement. "The least you could do is grease Leslie's 'sociability wheels,' maybe give her a few tips."

Bess sighed. She felt protective of Leslie. "She seems so helpless here," she muttered. "So alone, like a lost puppy."

"Wow," Brian said suddenly. "This is going to be good. He's—is he? . . ."

"Yep, he *is!*" Bess added, delighted.

She couldn't believe it: Some guy was actually hitting on her roommate.

"This is great," she said.

The next thing she knew, Leslie had set her plate down and followed the guy onto the dance floor.

To Bess's astonishment, Leslie was a pretty good dancer. "Good hip flex, limber arms," she said, surprised. "Not bad footwork. She doesn't know quite what to do with her head, but we can forgive her that. All she needs is a little bit of seasoning."

Shaking her head, Bess laughed. "I never thought I'd say that I'm happy for her, but I *am.*"

When the song was over, the guy said something to Leslie and Bess noticed he took her hand and held it a minute.

"He's definitely hitting on her," she concluded. "I'm needed."

"I'll say," Brian agreed. "You'd better give her some tips, fast, before she blows it."

"Wish me luck."

Brian shook Bess's hand. "Good luck."

Bess walked over toward Leslie as the guy

moved off toward the drinks table. She not-so-casually knocked into her. "Leslie, how terrific that you're here tonight," she said, acting surprised.

Leslie blushed and stammered. "I thought I'd drop by."

Bess's eyes traveled over her, from head to toe. She nodded approvingly. "Nice dress. Wherever did you get it?" she teased.

Leslie looked at her a second, not comprehending, then laughed as she caught on. Bess chuckled, too. Not *at* Leslie as much as *with* her. She'd never, in all these weeks of living together, seen her roommate smile so much.

"Well, I'm glad to see you changed your mind and came tonight," Bess said.

Leslie's eyes glittered—with affection, Bess guessed, though she couldn't be sure.

Wow, she's even pretty, Bess thought, admiring the way Leslie had let down her long brown hair, and even attempted a little lipstick.

Bess draped her arm over Leslie's shoulder. She felt Leslie tense up a second, then relax into it. Bess leaned her head in confidingly.

"So?" she asked.

Leslie seemed to be trying to figure out what Bess meant. "So—what? You mean the gambling? I actually won ten dollars playing craps, and I don't even know what craps *is!*"

Bess threw her head back in laughter, then settled. "No, I mean *this*—" She swiveled her hips and did a little dance step. "You can't fool me, Leslie King," Bess prodded her. "I saw you dancing out there with that towering hunk o' man."

A glimmer of a sly smile played across Leslie's lips. Her voice dropped to a confessional murmur. "He *was* pretty hunky, wasn't he?"

Bess grinned from ear to ear. She *loved* this. She and her roommate were actually gossiping!

Suddenly she wiped away her smile and her expression settled into one of deadly seriousness.

"Let me share with you just a few little pointers about men," she began. "The first rule of thumb is: It's a long life, a big pond, crowded with fish. You have to bait them with the utmost care. . . ."

"You guys look like you're having a blast," Paul said as George and Will collapsed, panting, into a couple of the chairs lining the wall.

The Beat Poets had just ended a set of Elvis's beach-blanket dance tunes. Bow ties were flying off all over the place as the evening moved on and things were loosening up. The band was getting louder. The gambling was picking up steam. And Sam was continuing to roll.

"I'm really, really impressed with this event," George said, nodding at the huge party. "Hey, we met your roommate, Paul. He's a nice guy."

"Is that Emmet Lehman I hear you talking

about?" Bess interrupted, stepping in. Paul tensed as she slid her arm around his waist.

"You okay?" she mouthed.

Paul patted his tuxedo pocket. "I have some money to get downstairs," he started to explain.

"Just estimate how many students are here tonight," Will was saying, "added to the money from those five-hundred-dollar tickets last night—and you should have a ton of money."

"Even *with* Mr. Blackjack," George threw in.

Paul winced. For a couple of minutes he'd managed to forget about Sam, and all the money he was draining from the charities. He took a furtive glance toward the blackjack table.

As if Sam will miraculously evaporate into thin air, he thought sardonically. *I wish.*

Bob gave him a wave from the door and came over. "Okay, boss. Mike and I are ready when you are."

"We have to go down and grab some more playing chips and plastic cups and stuff," Paul explained to Bess, George, and Will. "You guys have fun." He looked at Bess. "Go find Emmet and ask him to dance. He'd love that, and I know I haven't been much fun tonight."

Paul led Bob and Mike down into the basement. "Any problems?" he asked.

"Nope, everything's fine so far," Bob replied.

"A lot less money at the door," Mike added. "Then again, no one's paying five hundred dollars a pop, but I think the gambling tables are taking in more than last night."

Paul nodded. He thought so, too. They were doing okay. The thought gave him a little jolt of positive energy.

I have to make sure I get at least one dance in with Bess, he reminded himself.

They ducked into the storeroom and started filling paper grocery bags with the supplies.

"You're going to have to give the blackjack tables more chips," Paul said, annoyed. "Why don't you guys take that stuff up. I'll bring this last bag myself. I have to step into the office for a sec—I'll meet you upstairs."

Paul walked out of the storeroom with his fraternity brothers and watched them until they turned a corner. He walked down the hall and stepped into the small room they'd set up as the office. He took a wad of cash from his jacket pocket. Two handfuls of five- and ten-dollar bills.

I should have deposited that money last night, he silently scolded himself. Safe or no safe, that was incredibly dumb! No matter how much I wanted to be with Bess, or how tired I was. What if it's gone, and I've lost fifty *thousand* dollars?

Calm down, he commanded himself. No one even knows where this is. Or can get into it.

He could hear the lock click, and he opened the safe door. The locked strongbox felt heavy. At least that was a good sign.

He lifted the lid slowly.
The money was all there.

"That's the eighty-seventh time you spun Bankrupt on the wheel of fortune," a voice called out.

Liz whirled around. Daniel was standing with his arms folded across his chest. It was her first slow period. She'd had a steady stream of customers all night. But Daniel was the only person she really wanted to see.

"I think you need to give someone else a chance to spin," he said insistently.

"But what would I do if I took a break?" Liz wondered innocently.

Daniel wagged his fingers. "I've been watching you. You're stiffening up. In the shoulders particularly. I've consulted a committee of physicians, and they concur that the fact that you haven't danced at all, last night or tonight, is a potentially dangerous pattern of self-abuse. The consequences are just too terrifying to consider."

Liz struggled not to smile. "Really. And what does the committee suggest would remedy this perilous condition?"

Daniel nodded. "A stiff regimen of dancing. With me, of course. Since I'm most familiar with this ailment," he added quickly.

Liz buttonholed a friend to take over, then met Daniel on the dance floor, ready to cut loose. She had to admit, the idea of cutting loose did appeal to her.

Ray Johansson suddenly slowed the beat, and the band slid into a sexy ballad. It was exactly what she was hoping for. Daniel took her hands, opened her arms, and stepped between them. Then he closed her arms around his waist and started to dance slowly.

"How are you doing now?" Daniel asked.

Liz could feel herself wanting to fall into him. Her heart was racing. He was wearing the same cologne he had on when they first met, and when she smelled it now, it *was* Daniel. She'd missed it and him. And wanted them both back. It felt so good to have him back in her life.

"I'm doing just fine," she said, barely more than a whisper.

Daniel cleared his throat. "I missed you the past few weeks. It's been hard to see you and not be able to hold you. I'm glad we talked."

The lights dimmed, then darkened as Liz's eyes fluttered closed. The music floated her away, and the world was reduced to only Daniel's scent and the touch of his strong hands.

I missed you, too, she told him in her mind. I've missed your touch. But now that's far behind us.

Sighing, she leaned her head against Daniel's chest and felt him gently kiss her hair.

Almost imperceptibly they cinched their arms a little more snugly, tightening their embrace.

CHAPTER 9

"Okay, boys, hold on to your wallets," Nancy warned kiddingly. "Here comes the blackjack queen."

Nancy smiled as she approached the middle blackjack table, winking at Billy. Her gaze lingered on Sam's face. He returned her smile, chuckling.

"The competition was definitely getting too male," he said.

Jake looked annoyed and pushed away from the table, giving Nancy his seat.

Nancy made a big show of cracking her knuckles and limbering up her neck. "Ready," she announced, and Billy passed around the cards. Five minutes later Jake was nodding behind her shoulder.

"You're much better at this than I am," he admitted. "I lost twenty dollars in five minutes. You've only lost ten."

Nancy patted his hand. "That's because women are innately more intelligent than men," she explained soothingly. "Wouldn't you agree," she asked Sam.

"Sam Porter," he replied. He swept his hand over his neatly stacked towers of chips. "But I'm not sure I can agree with you."

"Yes, well, sometimes *getting* the money is only the beginning," Nancy suggested meaningfully. "What happens to it afterward is much more interesting."

Sam didn't miss a beat. "I agree. The fun only starts when you win."

Nancy smiled, but she still couldn't see a thing. What was Sam up to?

"Another?" he asked as he cleaned up on yet another hand.

Without commenting, Nancy leveled an inquiring look at him. He raised his eyes, matching the intensity of her gaze, but Nancy held steady. Sam blinked and slid his eyes away.

What are you up to? Nancy wanted to know. And how? Why? He obviously has plenty of money. Enough for a five-hundred-dollar ticket. He's a wealthy man's son.

Sam lost the next hand to Nancy, though she noticed he'd staked only the minimum, two dollars. "Wow, you *lost* two dollars!" she cried with mock horror, eyeing his pile of hundreds.

"Congratulations," he joked.

Jack and Glenn had appeared behind Sam. Glenn leaned down and whispered something in Sam's ear. Sam nodded, checked his watch, and shrugged. "I'll cash out now, thank you," he said to Billy.

Billy's jaw dropped, and he glanced at Nancy. The crowd began to murmur, and a couple of people even started to boo.

Nancy didn't get it. Why stop now? she wondered.

"But the evening is young," she said. *"I* certainly wouldn't stop if I were you."

Sam chuckled. "But you're not me, are you?"

Thankfully, Nancy replied in her head.

Sam sighed. "I have places to go, people to see. I appreciated the opportunity to hone my card-playing skills. Thank you."

Sam slid off his stool and waded into the crowd.

"You're welcome," Jake grumbled after Sam was out of earshot.

"Well, excuse me if *I'm* not," Nancy replied.

"But I'm glad that's over," Jake said. "Now, let's forget about him and his small band of flunkies, and dance. Ray's not going to play forever."

"He was doing something with those cards,"

Nancy said intensely, staring at the table. The crowd had thinned out. She lifted her eyes and watched Sam until he'd stepped through the exit and out of Hewlitt into the night.

"It's over," Jake replied. "Done. Forget it."

"I can't," she said. "He was unstoppable, yet he left. He didn't make as much as he could have. Why?"

Jake cocked his head. "Good questions. But why look a gift horse in the mouth?"

"Some horse," Nancy muttered. "All that money lost."

Jake grabbed the deck of playing cards that Billy had just put aside as he opened a fresh deck. He handed them to Nancy. "Here, take a look at these. Figure out what Sam was doing. But for now, let's just do some partying and have a good time."

As much as Nancy wanted to party with Jake, she couldn't. She peered at the cards and turned them over and over in her hand.

"Hey, you can't take those," Billy told her.

"You mind if I look at them?" Nancy asked.

Billy shrugged. "Just give them back by the end of the night. I have to pack my table up. Everything gets returned to the store tomorrow."

Nancy cut the deck and looked at a card. It was the two of clubs.

By then Jake's hand was on Nancy's wrist and he was kissing the back of her neck. He whispered in her ear, "Dance with me? Now. Please?"

Bess was winding down. She'd run out of actual gas hours ago and was on pure adrenaline now. But she was having so much fun dancing and watching Leslie practice Bess's suggested moves on the three or four guys who asked her to dance that there just wasn't time to be tired. I can always sleep, Bess decided. This night, which they'd all worked so hard for, was a hit—one hundred percent.

But now it was over. The Beat Poets were packing up. The Zeta men and Kappa women who still had energy were starting to tear down the sets. The dealers and croupiers were counting their cards and chips. And Holly Thornton was still strolling around with the green visor on her head.

Bess was giddy with fatigue as she chatted with Ray.

"So," Bess said, "did I ever tell you I always wanted to be a guitar player?"

"No, you didn't," Ray said, smiling as Ginny walked up, rolling wire from the soundboard around her shoulder and elbow.

"That's because you don't want to be a guitar player," Ginny reminded her as she passed.

"But I did want to play the drums!" Bess called after her.

She moved off and followed a trail of paper napkins and plates. She ended up at Paul's feet.

"Hey, you know that bag has a hole in it?" Bess pointed out.

Nancy, Jake, Liz, and Daniel started to laugh. Paul's shoulders sagged. He looked ready to pass out. Nancy grabbed the bag. "Why don't you do what you have to do, and let other people clean up?" she said.

Paul nodded wearily. "Good plan. You guys want to come down to the dungeon with me for a minute? I have a lot of of stuff to carry down there."

"Only if we can leave a trail of bread crumbs," Daniel joked.

Nancy held up the leaky plastic bag. "Will plastic forks do?"

Laughing, the group made their way toward the stairway carrying things that had to go back to the fraternity: plates, napkins, cups.

"You know what the best thing is?" Paul said, leading the way. "Mike told me that people had such a great time, that almost all of them donated whatever they'd earned tonight to charity."

"That should make up for our one card-playing weasel," Jake said.

Bess met Jake's eye and shook her head. She didn't want Paul to obsess over Sam anymore. It was all over, and the night had been a huge success. Paul had worked *so* hard! She squeezed his hand. "It *was* great, wasn't it?" she prodded.

Paul shrugged.

"I just want to hear you say it," she pressed him.

Reluctantly Paul nodded. "It went okay."

Daniel slapped him on the back. "Okay? It was awesome!"

"And the biggest winners were Helping Hands and the other campus groups," Bess said to Nancy, draping a loving arm around her old friend. "You did a great job helping organize. Thanks."

Nancy's hand shot up in the air like a traffic cop's. "Okay, okay. Enough with the compliments."

Everyone dropped their loads in the storeroom, then accompanied Bess and Paul to the office three doors away.

Paul opened the door to the office. Bess's eyes automatically went to the safe. She'd started thinking about the money a little while ago and knew she should have allowed Paul to deposit the cash the night before. Even if they were tired. But it didn't matter. Everything was fine.

"Let's leave the two lovebirds to make off with all our hard-earned money," Liz teased, clowning around.

"This way, troops," they heard Daniel call. "Only ten more miles to the surface!"

Bess shook her head. "It's wonderful that Daniel and Liz are back together. They make a great couple."

Paul nodded. "I caught them behind a door."

Bess growled playfully. "I'd like to catch *you* behind a door." She poked his sides, tickling him.

Paul laughed so hard he couldn't breathe. "Okay, okay. I give! Time for the money thing."

Bess arched an eyebrow. "I have something to confess. I was a bit worried all day—I sort of wish we hadn't left it all here."

"Me, too," Paul admitted, shaking his head. "But it's no problem. I checked a couple hours ago. It was all present and accounted for."

Bess breathed a sigh of relief. Walking back to the door, she felt something crunch under her feet.

"What's—" Bess looked down, and picked up a small metal circle. "What is that?" she showed Paul as he punched in the computer code for the safe lock.

"What? Oh, a cuff link, I guess. There, the nice click of a lock unlocking."

Bess laughed, holding the cuff link up to the light. "Jake keeps losing this dumb thing! It isn't even that nice. Not as nice as yours." She pocketed it to give to him later.

"The moment of truth," Paul finally said, opening the safe.

*   *   *

"Bess and Paul have been down there a long time," Nancy said, glancing at her watch. It was almost two in the morning. Everything was cleaned up. She, Jake, Daniel, and Liz were sitting around a table, polishing off half-empty bags of chips and opened bottles of soda.

"They're celebrating," Jake declared, clearing his throat. "In a manner of speaking."

Nancy eyed him. "You're so sure."

Jake shrugged. "Paul's a man. Bess is a woman. It's only natural."

"They're lost," Daniel deadpanned, throwing back a handful of chips. "I'm sure of it. We'll send a search party in the morning, though by then it'll probably be too late. There'll be nothing left but bones."

"I think if I drink another sip of this, I'm going to drown," Liz moaned.

Casey appeared in the doorway, her face still caked in her white Madonna makeup. Everyone gave her a round of applause. Charley followed her in, not looking particularly pleased.

"Where's Brian?" Nancy wanted to know.

Casey thumbed behind her. "Passed out in his room. He's exhausted."

"You guys had a great act there," Nancy said.

"Yeah, great," Charley said, rolling his eyes. "Casey not only *does* Madonna, she wants to *look* like her."

"What do you guys think?" Casey asked, primping her hair. "Platinum blond?"

"You *must* be kidding!" Liz cried.

"There they are. Finally!" Daniel announced.

Everyone turned. Paul and Bess were coming toward them across the dance floor. Their expressions were stunned, their faces white.

Nancy shot to her feet. "What is it!"

Paul silently held the cashbox in front of him, opened the lid, and turned it over. Everyone's eyes were on the box.

The box was empty.

"It's gone," Bess said, near tears. Nancy could see the dried mascara streaking down her face. She'd been crying.

"What happened?"

Paul dropped the box on the table with a clatter. "The lock was jimmied."

No one said a word. Everyone stared in stunned silence. Nancy stopped breathing. "*All* of tonight's money?"

But Paul's face was slack, his mouth a grim line.

"Most of it," Bess explained. "We still have the money from the last couple hours."

But it wasn't only this, Nancy could tell. There was more. "What about Friday's money?" she asked tentatively. "We still have that in the bank. Right? That was the bulk of it."

Tears ran down Bess's face as she turned to

Paul. He shook his head. "We totally blew it," he said. He couldn't lift his eyes. "All of it. Every penny. We didn't take the money to the night deposit last night."

Casey clamped her hand over her mouth. "Oh, no!" she said through her hand.

"None of it?" Nancy gasped. She couldn't believe it. "How much?"

"Fifty ... maybe sixty ..." Paul started to say.

". . . *thousand* dollars?" Jake finished.

"In cash and checks," Paul said.

Jake held his forehead. "Oh, man. Wow."

Nancy lowered herself slowly into her chair and looked around the room at all the party debris. At all their hard work. "But how?" she asked. "Wasn't the strongbox inside a locked safe?"

Paul nodded. "I don't know how someone got that open. It was still locked when I did the computer code just now."

"What happened last night?" Jake looked at Paul. "How come you didn't take the proceeds to the bank like you planned?"

Paul cleared his throat. "It's my fault," he said resolutely. "Bess and I were tired and ... well, never mind, it doesn't matter. We should have gone to the night deposit. It was my decision, totally."

"It doesn't matter now," Nancy said sorrowfully. "It's gone. We have to call the police—"

"The police?" a booming voice asked from the entrance.

Everyone turned. H. Samuel Porter and his wife were standing there, their coats draped over their arms, grinning.

Nancy winced and hid her eyes.

"I just wanted to come by to see how everything went tonight," Porter said, smiling. "I heard it was a huge success, and wanted to congratulate you all on a job well done. I thought, if you're not all too tired, you could all come to my home and have some refreshments."

Paul shook his head. "Sir, we have some bad news."

Nancy closed her eyes.

"The money's been stolen," Paul said calmly.

The smile slowly slipped from Porter's face as Paul told him the whole story. About how he blew off delivering the past night's earnings to the night deposit. How when he was downstairs only two hours ago, the strongbox was still locked and full. How just now he'd found the lock jimmied open, and everything gone.

"All those thousands of dollars!" Porter boomed slowly, enunciating every syllable.

Bess looked as if she would collapse any second. Instinctively Daniel and Jake rose and stood beside Paul.

Porter considered them all with hard, cold stares. His hands were shaking, but Nancy noticed his voice was under control, businesslike, though without a trace of his earlier warmth.

"As far as I'm concerned, everyone presently in this room is a suspect," he declared. "No one is to move." He turned to his wife. "Please call the police, dear," he said, then turned back to the group, his eyes blazing. "Before we go to sleep, we will get to the bottom of this!"

CHAPTER 10

Bob and Mike staggered up to the entrance of Hewlitt. The entire organization committee was being assembled by the police on the wide stone steps. Two officers were guarding them.

"What's up?" Mike asked, rubbing his eyes.

"Have a seat," Paul said. "They want to talk to you."

"Who wants to talk to us?" Mike grumbled.

"And why at four in the morning?" Bob complained.

Nancy watched grimly as the red and blue emergency lights on the police cars scissored up into the night. Flashlights stabbed through the dark along the perimeter of the Hewlitt Performing Arts Center. The police had scoured the downstairs office and the supply rooms, checking all the windows. Now they were combing the rest of the huge building.

Jake came back outside and plopped down beside Nancy.

"How'd it go?" she asked.

"The police chief was fine, but Porter made me nervous," Jake explained. "They asked me if I ever had access to the money, where I was at every second of the night, who was I with, if Paul had given me the computer code to the safe. Just being there made me feel guilty. I'm sure guilt was written all over my face."

"It's all over all our faces," Nancy replied wearily. "Porter practically accused me of taking the money and planning to run off with it."

"Yeah, well, that doesn't seem like such a bad idea," Jake grunted. "There're a lot of other places I'd rather be right now."

"I think it's crazy for us to be the only suspects," Daniel piped up angrily. "There were hundreds of people around the building. Upstairs and downstairs. What about the janitors? Where were they?"

"We were the only ones who saw the money," Bess replied. "Paul and I saw it more than anybody. They should just let you guys go home and get some sleep."

Nancy sighed. "I couldn't sleep right now if I tried."

Charley groaned out loud. He was stretched out on one of the marble steps, his arms folded over his eyes. "I can't believe I flew all the way from California to be ignored by my girlfriend, lose two nights' sleep, and see her accused of grand larceny!"

Casey was leaning back with her elbows up on the step behind her, her legs crossed, nervously bouncing one leg across her knee. "Your next trip will have to be better," she said dryly to Charley.

Charley snorted humorlessly. "Hah!"

"Here," Jake said, handing a small box to Nancy. "A little memento from our lovely evening. To remember Sam by."

Nancy looked down at a deck of cards in her hand, then put them away when she heard Porter's voice behind them. He was talking to one of the detectives. "Maybe the whole lot of them conspired to steal it," he was saying. "And if not all of them," Porter continued, "then definitely the boy who was supposed to be responsible for the cash."

Nancy shot to her feet. After all of Paul's hard work, she couldn't let Porter stand there and accuse him. "We're just as upset about this as you are," she insisted. "After all the work we put in."

Porter didn't blink or give a single sign that he'd heard her. He just turned to the detective and said, "Keep me informed," then marched through the group of people spread out along the steps toward his waiting limousine.

"You're free to go," the detective called out to Nancy and the others. "We'll probably be calling you in again, so don't leave campus without telling us. But go home and get some sleep."

"Yeah, right," Nancy heard Jake say as she watched Porter's car fade into the night.

Paul appeared behind her. "We should call Max Krauser."

Nancy winced. In all the confusion and hysteria, she'd forgotten about him. With all of his troubles at home, this was the last thing he needed with his mother so ill.

Nancy felt sorry for Paul because she knew he was tearing himself up inside. But he was right—he had blown it.

"I think I should call him and tell him myself," Paul said grimly.

Nancy nodded. "I think that's a good idea."

Ribbons of bright morning sunlight streamed into the lounge of Suite 301, smacking Charley in the face. The couch was worse than his bed at the motel—lumpier and smaller.

"Human beings aren't supposed to live like this," he muttered as he painfully sat up and blinked. He looked at his watch. "Wow, a whole three hours of sleep."

After the police let them go and Charley

walked Casey back to Thayer Hall, he was too tired to drive back to his motel. Everyone had sat up in the lounge, too upset and nervous to sleep. By the time they all finally went to their rooms, the sun was coming up. And since Stephanie didn't have any warning, and it was too late to find somewhere else to sleep, Charley slept on the couch.

A door creaked open down the hall. Stephanie staggered out, shielding her eyes, wearing a very short silk nightie. Charley tried not to look. But her hair looked peculiarly great for this early, and her face seemed suspiciously fresh. And Charley couldn't help observing her slim, scantily clad body.

Ignoring him, Stephanie started to sit down. Charley, who'd been sitting in the middle of the couch, scooted over just in time. Stephanie settled in, hanging her head and looking as distressed as Charley felt.

Neither said a thing.

"Want to tell me about it?" he asked, making conversation.

Stephanie stared at him sleepily. "I don't want to burden you. Besides, you don't look so hot yourself."

Charley sighed. "It's a long story."

"I bet it is. Does it have anything to do with the fact that Casey's never around but always seems to be rushing off here and there? Or that she's always making plans on the phone for a party, or something or other?"

Charley peered at her. "Thanks, Steph. I knew that to feel better about my relationship, all I had to do was talk to you."

The flickers of an I-told-you-so expression played across Stephanie's face. "Just wanted you to open your eyes," she said.

Charley sniffed. "What's that scent?"

"Eau de Stephanie," she replied with a syrupy French accent. "I had it made especially for me on vacation with my father in Cancun."

Charley eyed her dubiously. "French perfume in Mexico? And you wear it to bed?"

Stephanie waved a hand blithely in the air. "Speaking of bed, it's a shame you and Casey couldn't be together last night."

"It wouldn't have been fair to you," Charley replied.

"Me? Don't be silly, I wasn't born yesterday," Stephanie said. "Come to think of it, Casey never does seem to be in her own bed when you're not around. By the time I get up, she's always off to work out at the gym with some weight lifter or something."

Charley gritted his teeth. He didn't know what was making him madder—Stephanie's painfully obvious attempt at making him feel terrible about Casey, or the fact that she was succeeding. He *was* feeling terrible. Casey had been avoiding him all weekend. And he only had the most important thing in the world to say to her.

Drumming his fingers on his knee, Charley felt his mind start to race. His blood quickened at the thought of Casey in her skimpy workout clothes with some perfectly molded, muscled undergrad.

I know if *I* were in college, I'd go on *lots* of dates.

He swallowed. Is that what Casey is doing? Is *that* why she's avoiding me?

You're overreacting, bud, he told himself. You know that Stephanie's a pro at making herself feel better by making everyone around her feel worse. You know that half of what she spews is always a lie.

"Then again," he mumbled under his breath, doing the simple math in his head, "half of it isn't."

Nancy woke late and ran down for a quick brunch in the cafeteria before it closed. When she returned to the suite upstairs, the first thing she saw was Charley. He was finally awake—and backed into one corner of the couch by Stephanie, who was practically in his lap! He didn't seem very happy, and Nancy wasn't surprised. Stephanie looked as if she was giving him the full-court flirt.

Although he's probably used to suffering

through beautiful women throwing themselves at him, Nancy thought with a chuckle.

The worst thing of course was that Stephanie knew better. Charley's girlfriend was her own roommate.

Don't even begin to try to figure her out, Nancy told herself. That's the Stephanie we've all come to know and—well, *know*.

Nancy was just passing the table in front of the couch when her eye fell on a torn piece of paper. She could see her initials along the top.

"Stephanie?" Nancy asked. "Is that for me by any chance?"

"What?" Stephanie asked sharply, obviously annoyed that Nancy was interrupting her little powwow with Charley. She glanced at the piece of paper. "Oh, yeah, right. Some guy called for you this morning."

"Thanks," Nancy replied with a sigh. It was amazing how Stephanie managed to find ways to annoy her. And not giving Nancy a phone message was one of them. Nancy was *almost* used to it, but still, it was a drag.

She grabbed the piece of paper and tried to decipher it. Party store, signature, not necessary, money.

"Stephanie?" Nancy grinned. "I'm really sorry to bother you again, but do you think you could maybe *explain* this to me a little bit?"

Stephanie huffed and turned to face her.

"Some guy from Collegetown Party Supply called to tell you that no one signed off on the supply inventory for the big charity do-dah, which is necessary if you want to get back any of the deposit." She stopped to breathe and arched a brow. "Okay? Are we done? Any more questions?"

Nancy stifled a laugh. "Thanks, Stephanie. I can't imagine why it wasn't clear from your note."

Waving her fingers dismissively, Stephanie turned her attention back to Charley.

Nancy stuck the piece of paper in her pocket. Last night the Zeta brothers had done a great job gathering up all the supplies to return to the rental place.

But Nancy wasn't surprised that no one had remembered to sign the receipt confirming that everything was being returned undamaged. The rental place had picked up the stuff because they needed it to go out to another customer for that night, Sunday. They must have noticed the missing signature then.

Nancy went to her room to grab her car keys and a jacket. The deposit had been a pretty good amount of money. And, Nancy thought sadly, they couldn't afford to lose any more money than they already had.

Twenty minutes later she was downtown at Collegetown Party Supply. She had to knock to get in because the store was officially closed. A burly guy let her in, then went back to flipping through stacks of papers.

Nancy waited for him to take a break, and when he didn't, she cleared her throat.

The guy paused and looked up.

"I'm Nancy Drew," she explained. "You left a message for me about a form we didn't sign for Black and White Nights?"

"Oh, yeah," the burly man said, pushing the stack of papers aside and fishing a stapled collection of pink receipts from a tray to his left.

"Just come back with me," he said, walking ahead. "Then I'll give this back to you to sign and I can release the deposit."

Nancy followed him into the back of the store. Two Collegetown trucks were pulled up to an open garage door in back. Some of the tables and chairs were still stacked in the back of the truck and there were a number of bags and boxes on the cement floor around it.

"You should have signed this last night. We checked over the order ourselves," the burly guy said. "But just take a quick look and make sure nothing's missing."

Nancy nodded and picked her way over to the pile of stuff. There were the felt table covers, the white tablecloths, the green cloth napkins. There were open boxes filled with plastic bags of chips, and plastic card deck holders, trays, and coasters.

Nancy scanned the truck and saw the long banquet tables and round tables they'd rented for the food and the card games. And there were about a million chairs stacked up all over the place.

For a second she just couldn't believe that the whole thing was over. It had taken so much planning and energy. It had been excellent, too, until it all blew up in their faces.

"So you didn't need the cards," the clerk said, nodding. "I always think it's a good idea to order some anyway, like you did. That way you're never in a jam."

"What are you talking about?" Nancy replied. "We used the cards you sent us."

The man scratched his head. "You did? Because when we checked the order, we found this box—"

He showed Nancy a box that was still tightly taped up. There was a black stamp across the tape on top of the box—Regulation Playing Cards: 100 Deck Count.

Uh-oh, Nancy thought. I don't like the look of this.

"See what I mean?" the guy asked. "This was the only box of cards that went out on the truck, and it came back to us on the truck."

"Maybe it's a mistake," Nancy said.

The guy shrugged. "Usually we just give away used cards after a party," the guy explained. "Because once a deck is opened, we aren't allowed to sell it again. But these were never used. Look," he said, pointing to the seal.

"Was there another box of cards?" Nancy asked, knowing it wasn't true even as she suggested it.

The guy checked the order form. "Nope. Just one box. A hundred decks. Even if you didn't use all of them, you would have at least opened the box." The guy shrugged again.

"But we had more than enough cards for both nights," Nancy said.

The clerk sighed. "The kid who was supposed to be taking care of all this stuff has been a little out of it lately. Somehow he wrangled himself a couple of tickets for that party of yours. It's all he talked about. But he swore to me he'd take care of all this. 'No problem,' he said."

Nancy looked surprised. "Your delivery guy was there?"

"Yeah. Must've done okay gambling 'cause when he dropped off one of those trucks out there this morning I was worried his grin was going to split his face."

"Do you think you could tell me about him?" Nancy asked. "Just out of curiosity. Though I probably didn't see him, there were so many people."

"Sure," the burly guy said. "Blond-haired kid. Quiet. Knowles is his name. Jack Knowles."

Nancy's pulse picked up. "Jack," she repeated.

"Yeah, Jack. He's a joker, that one. I'll have to talk to him about this. But you say that you did have cards, right? So no problem."

"Right," Nancy said slowly. "No problem."

Except that Nancy *had* seen Jack at the Black & White Nights. More than once. And he had a few particular friends who had kept Nancy's attention all weekend. And their names were Sam and Glenn.

And if Jack didn't deliver the cards we ordered from Collegetown, she thought, exactly whose cards did he deliver?

CHAPTER 11

Bess was sitting on the steps outside Thayer Hall, hugging her knees. She knew she had a ton of work to do. She had quizzes in three classes, and she was just getting on top of everything. Thanks to Ginny, who had been her unofficial tutor, she was actually pulling B's in biology.

But right now she couldn't even contemplate cracking a book. She was obsessed. She had to talk to Nancy and tell her the news.

"Why is it that whenever something wonderful happens, like Black and White Nights," she pondered out loud, "something awful has to steamroll right over it?"

Shielding her eyes from the sunlight, Bess spotted Nancy walking up the walk.

"Nancy!" she cried, leaping to her feet.

"Bess! Guess what—"

But Bess's news had been on the tip of her tongue all morning, and it came spilling out first. "Porter filed a complaint against Paul two hours ago," she said breathlessly. "They're pressing charges. Porter claims he has a witness."

Nancy looked at her, waiting, then asked, slowly, "A witness who saw what?"

Bess shrugged. "Paul leaving the office with a big bag during the party?"

She winced as Nancy's jaw fell open.

"Well, *did* he leave with a bag?" Nancy asked.

Bess bristled with a surge of indignation, grappling with a sudden urge to defend Paul at all costs. "I don't know," she responded quickly.

"But did he admit to it?"

Bess glared at her. "Look, I came for your help, not for you to call him a thief," she blurted out. "Wasn't it you saying we had to stick together last night?"

Nancy paused, then nodded. "Okay. I'm sorry. You're right. I'm just a little tense right now."

Bess breathed a sigh of relief. "Nancy, you just have to believe him. I couldn't take it if you thought he was guilty."

Nancy gave Bess's knee an affectionate squeeze. "So who's this supposed witness?"

"Porter says it's that kid Glenn. That friend of Sam's with the funny black hair. He says he was downstairs looking for the bathroom when he saw Paul leaving the office with a bag."

Nancy stared at Bess, as if she was thinking about something.

"What is it?" Bess asked. "What's wrong?"

"I was just remembering how confusing it was downstairs," Nancy wondered aloud. "I didn't see any bathrooms near the office." She shrugged. "Maybe I didn't notice."

"But the worst part," Bess continued, "is that the police pulled Paul out of bed this morning. In front of his entire frat. It must have been so humiliating! Nancy, they took him down to the station house for questioning!"

"You okay?" Emmet, Paul's beefy football player roommate, asked.

Paul slowly, reluctantly raised his head. He and Emmet were sitting in the lounge of Zeta house. All of the stuff from the weekend that hadn't been rented was piled neatly around him: the stacks of visors and plates; platters of leftover food covered in aluminum foil and scattered on the tables.

"I'm okay," Paul said, his voice steady and monotone. "I just want some time to myself. Thanks."

"No problem," Emmet replied, giving him a thumbs-up. "If you need anything, let me know. We're all behind you."

Paul managed a weak smile. "Thanks."

The fact was, Paul couldn't have felt worse. He'd just made two horrible phone calls. First, he'd called Max Krauser at home and told him about the missing money. Max seemed to take it pretty well, though Paul knew he had more important things on his mind right then. His mother wasn't doing very well. They didn't think she was going to make it, and Paul felt rotten about heaping more awful news on top of that.

Then he called his parents, not to tell them how great the entire weekend had gone, but to get him a lawyer.

And boy, did Mom love that, Paul said to himself, repeating the entire conversation in his mind.

Paul fought down a new wave of emotions as he remembered the horror of finding the empty strongbox, and then the trauma of having to face his friends with the news.

Paul sniffed. "Wow, this stinks," he said, his voice cracking.

The sunlight in the doorway was cut off. Paul raised his head, half expecting the police to be standing there again.

"Bess!" he said, relieved. He laughed sadly. "I thought it was the police."

Bess ran over and hugged him around the neck. "I'm so glad you're back. I brought Nancy and Jake. We wanted to know how it went."

Paul shrugged. "About as well as it could when you're dragged out of bed by the police and paraded in front of the entire university."

Nancy cleared her throat. "I was just wondering why you didn't tell us about going downstairs during the party."

Paul smiled. "You know what's funny? I didn't say anything because I thought everyone already knew! I went down three or four times each night. I was worried about keeping so much money in the cashbox, so I emptied it every couple of hours and put it in the strongbox in the safe. And Saturday night I went down an extra time because I was worried about something like this happening. I was feeling terrible about not depositing the money Friday night and wanted to make sure everything was okay."

"And did you tell that to the police?" Jake asked.

Paul threw up his hands. "Of course I told them. I even told them Mike and Bob could vouch for me. They saw me go down there. And Daniel—he was with me for a while. But the police are much more interested in getting me to admit I stole the money than in finding out the truth. I bet Porter's behind that. He's convinced I took the money because I was the only person besides him who knew the code for the safe's lock."

"Maybe *he* took the money," Jake murmured acidly.

"He doesn't exactly need it," Nancy said sarcastically. "So what *was* in the bag that Glenn said he saw you holding?" Nancy wanted to know.

Paul laughed. "Real illegal stuff." He waved his hands around him at all the plastic-wear lying around. "This," he said. "After Bob and Mike and I dropped it off, I sent them up and ducked into the office to check up on the money. Besides, one thing I don't get is, if I had the code to the computer lock on the safe, and the key to the strongbox all the time, why would I have to break open the strongbox?"

"That's easy," Nancy replied. "So everyone would think it was someone else. Not that it *was* you," she added quickly. "That's just what the police are thinking."

Paul nodded. "Okay, I can buy that. But there you go. See? I couldn't even think of that by myself. I have nothing to hide. I'm cooperating with them as much as I can. Though it seems pointless. When I give them my fingerprints, of course they'll be everywhere."

"But so will Daniel's," Bess countered. "And mine—I was down there, too."

"And mine," Nancy added.

Jake shrugged. "Mine, too. So what does that prove?"

Paul laughed sorrowfully. "According to Porter, that we're all guilty." He sighed and kicked his feet up on the table. "I sure hope my parents get me that lawyer."

He peeled back the foil on a tray of day-old sandwiches. "Yum," he remarked unenthusiastically. "Anybody hungry?"

"Shove over."

Nancy hip-checked Jake over to the left half of his seat at the *Wilder Times* office. It was early evening, when everyone at the paper was often busy doing last-minute editing and layout for Monday morning's edition. Most of the desks were full. The air was filled with the quiet clicking of computer keyboards and the whirring of printers.

Nancy squinted at Jake's monitor. "Is this the editorial you're supposed to have done by tomorrow?" she asked.

"The editorial I didn't have time to work on this weekend because some spunky gorgeous reporter kept me busy on another story?" Jake chuckled.

He pecked another sentence into his computer, paused, frowned, and then deleted it. He typed for another minute, then cleared his throat.

" 'The Citizens for White Purity is a bold new group that is making its presence felt on campus. C.W.P. has begun an avid propaganda campaign to spread its doctrine of complete separation of ethnic groups to keep the white race pure.' "

Jake paused and scratched his chin. "Well? What do you think?"

"Pretty intense." Nancy nodded. "I've seen them at one of their rallies. They sound scary."

"Yeah," Jake agreed. "But freedom of speech and all that. Right, Reporter Drew?" He chuckled again. "But that's why I have the freedom to skewer them."

"I wish I had the freedom to skewer whoever stole our money." Nancy sighed, examining the playing cards fanned out across her desk.

"Same here," Jake said.

"And I'd also like to get that jerk who cheated at the blackjack table."

"Sam was definitely a drag," Jake agreed, his eyes still glued to his computer screen. "But we still don't have any proof that he was cheating."

"Oh, come on," Nancy said. "Where's your reporter's gut instinct? You really don't think it's too much of a coincidence that Sam's friend works for the rental supply place? And that their cards were never used?"

Nancy checked the deck of cards in front of her again. It was the deck Jake had given her the night before. She'd never gotten a chance to give the cards a closer look. "I bet that box of cards from Collegetown wasn't even taken off the truck."

"You got someone else's cards," Jake said, still typing.

"Exactly," Nancy agreed, plucking a playing card from the deck. "We got these." Nancy flipped the card over and saw she held the jack of diamonds. "Another coincidence?" she murmured. "I don't think so. These are the cards that Sam was so *lucky* with. And I just can't believe in that much luck."

"Well, excuse me for disagreeing with you," Jake said, stopping to turn and lean over to her. He put his hands on either side of her face. "*I* can believe in that much luck," he said, gazing into Nancy's eyes. "I met you, didn't I?"

Nancy's eyelashes fluttered closed and Jake brought his lips to hers. With a sigh she leaned into him and let the turbulent thoughts of the weekend disappear. Jake pulled away, and Nancy saw he had a satisfied look on his face. Probably because it always took her a few minutes to collect herself after one of his kisses.

"I can't believe you can still do that to me," she said with a grin.

"Do what?" Jake asked innocently, all business again as he turned back to his story.

"Oh, you know. Make my heart pound, make my head spin, make me forget where I am. Even who I am," Nancy joked. "You're right, though. I guess that's no big deal. Pretty usual, in fact."

"Oh, no, Nancy Drew," Jake smiled back at her wickedly. "Nothing about us is usual."

"Okay, okay," Nancy agreed. "Anyway, thanks for your generous, though brief, lesson on luck. With us, I'll concede your point. But back to Sam and his friends"—Nancy shook her head—"no way."

Nancy flipped through the deck of cards again.

"Maybe you're just trying too hard?" Jake suggested. "You may not be aware of this, but there is such a thing as concentrating too much."

"I can just picture you giving that excuse to one of your high school teachers. 'Sorry, Mr. Jones, but haven't you ever heard of the TMC syndrome—Too Much Concentration?'" Nancy laughed as she leaped from her chair. Jake made a grab for her.

"Don't mock me," he warned with a teasing glint in his eyes as he caught her around the waist. "Haven't you ever seen those visual puzzles that are like three-D pictures if you see them the right way?"

"Yeah. So . . ." Nancy smiled and snaked her arms around Jake's neck.

"I tell you, Drew," Jake said, leaning in to kiss her, "you are very, very distracting. Perhaps even dangerous to my career." Suddenly Jake released her and stepped back. "Anyhow, the trick to all those things is to try *not* to focus on them. You're supposed to stare at them, and when your brain

is about to fry, you kind of look away and then—
ta-da!—you see the thing in the corner of your
eye."

Nancy grinned.

"Something like that, anyway," he said. "But
don't smirk. The way you're staring at those
cards, it's like you expect the answer to leap out
and hit you over the head."

"I'll hit you over the head if you don't get
more helpful," Nancy said, waving her fist at
him menacingly.

"Sure," Jake replied, sitting back at his desk
with the pages of his article and a red pen.

Nancy plopped back in her chair and picked
up her cards again. Maybe she *was* looking too
hard. After all, she hadn't seen Sam staring at
the cards, so if they were marked, it must be the
kind of thing that was easy to see. Once you
knew what you were looking for.

"So what am I looking for?" Nancy wondered.

She tried Jake's advice, looking at her knee, at
her fingers, trying hard to keep the card in her
sight without focusing on it. But nothing happened. Except that she started to get a headache.

Then she tried staring at the card again, looking at every line, until the red design on its back
started to swirl.

Why do I think the answer's just going to jump
right out at me? Nancy sighed to herself. Who
am I kidding?

Nancy was just about to give up when she actually thought she did see something in the corner of her eye. She looked again at the card in her hand, but couldn't find anything unusual.

But it's there, she prodded herself. I just saw it.

Again, she tried to put the card away, letting her gaze skate over the back of it.

There it was again! There was something on the back. She could almost recognize it. Something in the corners where red-etched flowers and vines made up the design.

She looked quickly at the card and then away, then back again, slowly, letting her gaze glide over it.

"I've got it!" she cried, turning to Jake excitedly. "Here, take these. Ask me any of them. Any of them."

"Okay, okay, just hold on." Jake took the cards and turned his back on Nancy. She could see he was shuffling them again. He turned to face her with the rest of the deck still behind his back. One card was pressed against his chest, facedown.

"Nine of diamonds," Nancy said before he could even ask.

Jake took the card from his chest and dropped the nine of diamonds onto his desk. He pulled another card out.

"Three of clubs," Nancy called out before he even stopped moving it.

"Queen of spades. Two of diamonds. Four of hearts. Six of spades. Kings of hearts." Nancy ran through the cards that Jake flashed at her.

"I knew it!" Nancy cried. "I knew something was going on!"

Jake nodded. "Wow. You've got it figured, all right."

"Look!" Nancy said excitedly, showing him the upper two corners of a card. Knowing what to look for made the difference, and now the marked deck was so clear to Nancy, it was almost embarrassing to realize she hadn't seen it before.

"On the left side, you can see in this pattern of vines and stuff, there's the outline of a number. Or a letter if it's a jack, queen, king or ace."

Nancy put her finger on the back of a card and traced out the faint outline of a seven.

"And here on the right side, it shows what suit the card is," Nancy said, drawing out the familiar shape of a heart.

"Way to go!" Jake cried, turning to give her a high five. "You're amazing. Let's take this show on the road. I think we've got some guys to see."

"Yep," Nancy agreed. "Tomorrow we'll pay our first visit to our friend Jack Knowles."

CHAPTER 12

Nancy craned her neck, scanning the Monday lunchtime crowd that packed Java Joe's. All the tables were taken, littered with coffee cups, half-eaten bagels, and editions of the latest *Wilder Times*. Nancy nodded in time to the beat of music playing on the boom box behind the counter.

Turn it up! she thought to herself, straining to hear the music above the conversational buzz. Anything to distract her from thinking about what had happened Saturday night or hear what people were saying about it. Every now and then, though, she couldn't help overhear someone talking about the police cars at Hewlitt and the theft. The headline across the front page of the *Wilder Times* read, "Charities Ripped Off!"

Thankfully, the story hadn't mentioned anyone by name, because no one had been officially arrested yet. But Nancy knew that rumors in college were more contagious than the common cold. It was no secret who the suspects were.

"Well, *I* heard that the guy from Zeta planned the whole thing from the start," Nancy overhead someone behind her saying, between bites of a bagel.

"Zeta's such a bunch of goons," her friend responded. "I'm not surprised."

Nancy moaned. "Poor Paul."

Slinging her knapsack over her shoulder and tugging down on the brim of her maroon W.U. baseball cap, she headed for the counter, hoping no one would recognize her.

"Double espresso," she ordered.

"One cup rocket fuel comin' up," the counter guy repeated back to her.

"Make that two!" a voice called out.

"Three!" someone else joined in.

George and Will slipped in next to Nancy.

Nancy groaned. George frowned in sympathy.

"Things really that bad?" Will asked.

Nancy nodded. "Worse." She managed a strained smile. "Paul has already been tried and convicted about a hundred times. But things could be looking up. You guys have a table? I'll fill you in."

"Will snagged the booth by the door," George said, nodding her head.

Suddenly a sardonic smile played at the corners of Nancy's mouth as she stared across the room. "Well, well," she said.

George craned her neck, searching eagerly. "What?"

"I'll meet you at your table," Nancy said. "Give me ten minutes."

Nancy twisted her way through the crowd, ducking beneath a guy carrying a tray full of orange juice and coffees. "Sam, right?" she said, walking up to a table with three guys.

"What?" Sam Porter said, lifting his eyes from the table. A deck of cards sat in the middle of the table. Each of the three guys had two cards in front of him, one down and one faceup. Nancy noticed that Sam's friends slouched, their faces drawn down. Sam, on the other hand, seemed as happy as ever. Which was no great shock to Nancy: Neat stacks of matches stood at attention in front of him, while the other guys had a few sticks scattered around the table.

"Blackjack," Nancy said laconically. "Surprise, surprise."

She stole a quick glimpse at the cards. They were the same as the ones she had and probably the same as the ones from Friday and Saturday night. The same marked cards, Nancy thought.

"Your luck still as good as it was all weekend?"

An embarrassed smile spread across Sam's face. He wagged his finger. "Nancy?"

Nancy nodded. "Good memory. I'm one of the people who watched you beat the pants off the dealer at Black and White Nights this weekend. I, unfortunately, wasn't such a winner."

Sam shrugged. "You win some and you lose some."

"Watch out for this guy," Nancy said to Sam's unfortunate friends. "He's good."

"No kidding," one of them muttered, tossing a melancholy glance at Sam's collection of matches and his own piece of pitifully bare table.

"Well, see you around." Nancy gave a little wave. "And watch your pockets!"

"Yeah, see ya," Sam replied, obviously relieved to see Nancy going.

Nancy stepped back, then stopped, snapping her fingers as if she'd forgotten something.

"Oh, *I* remember what I wanted to ask you!" she said enthusiastically. "You know, I was just thinking—most people ended up donating their winnings to the fund-raiser. And I just thought that, well, since you can obviously afford it now, maybe you'd consider donating some of *your* winnings." She smiled flirtatiously. "I just thought you seemed like the generous type."

But Sam didn't skip a beat. "I guess you need

it now that you lost everything else," he said without a trace of regret or sympathy.

Nancy gritted her teeth. She forced herself to smile. "You might say that," she said.

"Well, I hate to burst your bubble, but I already have a favorite charity."

"World aid? Human Habitat?"

Sam stared at her. *"Me."*

Nancy looked at him in disbelief. "How *kind* of you," she replied. She peered at the deck of cards. Since they were marked just like the others, and she knew how to read them, she could tell that the next card was a three. One of the guys Sam was playing against had eighteen and only needed a three to get to twenty-one to beat Sam's hand.

Nancy squinted and pressed her finger to her forehead. "You know," she said to the guy, "I'm getting this really strong transmission. I get them sometimes, I don't know from where. But I just got this really weird feeling that if you take just one more card, you'll beat this guy."

Everyone at the table exchanged looks. "What are you talking about?" Sam asked, squirming in his seat.

But Nancy shrugged. "I couldn't really say. It's just one of those weird feelings, just one of those things. Go ahead. Take the next card."

"But I already have eighteen," the guy said.

"Anything over a three and I'll be over twenty-one."

"What do you have to lose," Nancy said, "another matchstick?"

Hesitantly the guy picked up the next card and peeked at it. Then he slapped it down. "Blackjack!" he cried, grinning. He looked up at Nancy in amazement. "How did you know?"

Nancy leveled a knowing glare at Sam. "It's all in the cards. Depending on which cards you're using, that is."

Sam's head snapped up, a flicker in his eye. Then he laughed it off.

Nancy winked. "Be seeing you," she said, and gave Sam a parting pat on the shoulder.

"If I have one more slice of pizza, you're going to have to roll me out of here!" Ginny moaned as she clutched her stomach at the Beat Poets' garage rehearsal space.

"Well, we have plenty of pizza boxes," Ray joked. "I guess we can rig up some sort of stretcher."

Ginny leaned over and planted a wet kiss on Ray's cheek.

The band's drummer, Spider, grinned and shook his head.

"You know, I was thinking—" Ginny began.

"The answer is 'no,'" Ray answered.

Ginny laughed. "But you don't know what I was going to say."

"I do know that look you get in your eye. The last time you had that look, you had this great idea that we should try to get on the late-night talk shows."

Ginny shrugged, her lips pursed. "I still think you should do late-night TV—but that's not what I was going to say. I *was* going to say, before I was so rudely interrupted, that if you needed money, you could go to Vegas as an Elvis impersonation band." Ginny could barely contain her laughter.

Ray threw up his hands. "See what I mean? *Another* brilliant idea! I repeat: N-O!"

"Admit it, Ray, it *was* fun," Spider said. "And you *do* do a good Elvis."

"One day I'd like to do a good Ray Johansson," Ray said. "I want us to stay focused. We're going places. I can feel it. Elvis is for laughs. I don't want to be a comic."

Ginny admired him. Ray was the most driven human being she'd ever known. And the most talented. And beautiful, with his dark hair and buttery brown eyes, she thought he looked exactly like what he was—an up-and-coming star.

"What a bummer about the money from the fund-raiser, huh?" Spider said.

"But we got good exposure," Ray replied. "One of the trustees said he had a friend of a friend in the record business. He said he'd say something nice."

Ginny nodded. "I'd say you're probably going to get more gigs out of this. Definitely the W.U. radio station is going to pick up some of your stuff. But you can't depend on anyone else. You have to sell yourselves. What do you think about recording a few Elvis covers?" she joked.

"Have another piece of pizza" was Ray's droll reply.

"Want to know what I think?" Spider asked.

"Only if it's what I think," Ray muttered.

Spider ignored him. "*I* think Ginny should be our manager."

Ginny felt Ray's head swing in her direction. He was smiling mischievously. "Spider," he said, "now, *that's* a great idea!"

Ginny held up her hands. "Whoa, guys. Now, hold on."

"Oh, but you have all these great ideas!" Ray said with mock seriousness. "Vegas and Elvis and the radio station. 'Sell yourself,' you say. You're a natural!"

"A moron could see that you guys are going to be big," Ginny protested.

She looked at Ray, remembering what a trauma it was when her parents had found out they were going out. They'd envisioned someone for their daughter who was possibly premed and definitely Asian-American. But instead, they got a tattooed rock singer from a small farm town in the Midwest.

"Besides," Ginny continued. "I've been doing a lot of thinking lately about possibly changing majors from premed to something more liberal artsy. This would fit right in."

Ray nodded. "Uh-oh. I knew this was coming."

"So what do you say we just keep this little brainchild to ourselves for a while?" Ginny suggested. "Unless I want to put my parents in the hospital with heart attacks!"

"Are you ready?" Jake asked.

Nancy nodded. "I guess."

They were standing in front of Jack Knowles's dorm room. Jake had spent the last hour at the housing office getting this address.

Nancy had just finished telling him about seeing Sam in Java Joe's. And unless Sam was an idiot, he had to know that they were onto him and his friends. Jake just hoped he hadn't had a chance to call Jack and warn him.

"Okay," Nancy said, her eyes glittering.

Jake nodded and knocked sharply on the door. The door opened and Sam's friend Jack Knowles stood in front of them. He saw Nancy first and started to smile. But when he noticed Jake standing there, too, the smile slipped into a quizzical frown.

"Hi," Jake said, stepping forward. Jack fell

back into his room. "We just wanted to ask you a few questions."

"Questions?" Jack was saying. "About what? What is this?"

"You work at Collegetown Party Supply, right?" Nancy said brightly. "I'm from the Black and White Nights committee and I just wanted to clear up a few things."

"About what?" Jack asked nervously, shoving his hands into his pockets.

Jake saw that Nancy was staring at a small bookshelf against the wall. When he followed her gaze, he saw a collection of manuals on gambling and card-playing.

"I remember seeing you at the blackjack table," Nancy chatted on, "but you never played a single hand. Seeing all these books, I was about to ask you why, but I guess I don't have to." Nancy paused to study him closely. "I know why you didn't play," she said, her voice lowering conspiratorially.

"You do?" Jack asked, swallowing nervously.

"It was Sam, wasn't it?" Nancy said forcefully.

Suddenly all the color drained from Jack's face. "I don't—I don't know what you mean," he managed to choke out.

"Your friend Sam," Nancy said airily. "I mean, who would want to play at the same table with him? How could you hope to win when he was having such a lucky night?"

"Lucky?" Jack asked.

"Of course the cards must have helped," Jake added, looking at Nancy. "Right?"

"Oh, of course," Nancy agreed, smiling back at him. "It was the cards after all." Nancy turned to Jack. "Isn't that right? Wasn't it the cards?"

"I don't know anything about the cards," Jack said quickly.

"That's weird," Nancy said. "Because when I was down at Collegetown, they had the box of cards we'd ordered, just sitting there. Unopened. Your boss told us that you loaded the trucks. We just wondered if you knew anything about the cards that we actually did use."

"It must have been an extra box," Jack replied. "I guess I made a mistake. I'm sorry," he said. "Now I can't talk anymore. I've got a class soon."

Jake had been trying to circle the room casually, his reporter's eye searching for any sign of another set of cards. But Jack motioned for them both to move to the door.

"Well, I still have a deck," Nancy said as Jack practically pushed them into the hall. "I wasn't very good at cards, but since I've been playing with that deck, I feel I know a lot more about cards. I seem to be able to tell exactly what I'm going to get. Isn't that funny?" Nancy asked.

A frightened expression crossed Jack's face. Then he slammed the door in their faces.

"Well?" Jake asked. "That seemed pretty successful, don't you think?"

"I sure do," Nancy said, her eyes narrowing. "Something was definitely going on with the cards, and he knows about it."

Following Nancy down the hall, Jake could barely restrain himself. All he wanted to do was take her in his arms.

We really were amazing, Nancy and I, he thought admiringly. Cool as cucumbers.

"We've got to turn them in," Nancy said. "At least we'll be able to recover that money."

"But it's all still circumstantial evidence," Jake replied.

"But what about the marked cards?" Nancy pointed out. "That's not circumstantial."

"But, Nance," Jake reminded her. "There's only one person who has a deck of those cards. And that's you! The box of cards that was used at Black and White Nights is gone. We can't prove that all the cards used that night were marked."

"But Sam has a deck, too. The rest of the cards have to be somewhere," Nancy argued. "I'm sure Jack knows where they are."

Jake nodded. "He probably does. But if those cards aren't hidden or destroyed by now, they will be soon. Sam knows you're onto him. Now so does Jack."

"Sam won because he used a marked deck," Nancy pressed.

"But without the cards we can't prove that, either," Jake said.

"We have to confront them," Nancy argued. "We'll have to tell someone. Porter. Someone."

"Porter?" Jake asked, aghast. "Do you really think we can go to Porter and tell him we think his son won money by cheating, when we have nothing but circumstantial evidence and one deck of cards we could have gotten anywhere? It's *our* friend who's been accused of stealing *and* who had the computer code to the lock on the safe. Paul looks just as guilty."

Nancy was pensive.

"And now we want to accuse Sam, Porter's own son, and his friends, one of whom is the witness against Paul? No one else will believe us," Jake finished.

"But there's got to be something we can do!" Nancy said determinedly. "If we can't nail Sam until Paul is cleared, then we've just got to find out who stole the money."

"We've got to do that anyway," Jake agreed. For Paul's sake, at least, he thought.

Nancy pushed open the door to an on-campus snack shop, the Cave, and sighed as she entered its dark interior. She'd been preoccupied since her visit to Jack's dorm room. Even so, she had to remind herself she was also a student, which was why she'd spent the last hour trying to get some work done in the library.

But this time the quiet, studious atmosphere of the Rock and her upcoming quiz in journalism still weren't enough to keep her concentration on school. She couldn't stop thinking about Sam and his friends cheating and draining off all that money from the fund-raiser, which would have been stolen anyway, she remembered. At least if they could recover Sam's money, they might make something.

Nancy's stab at studying for the day was a bust. In an hour she was supposed to meet Bess at Hewlitt. She'd thought that maybe a break and a cup of coffee would make her feel a little better.

Nancy really loved the Cave. It was mostly filled with fine arts and architecture students, who always seemed to be working around the clock.

As soon as her eyes adjusted to the dark little snacketeria, Nancy was happy to see people she knew at a table in the corner. Liz and Daniel were sitting across from each other, their heads bent close together as they leaned over their coffees.

"Hey, you two," Nancy said as she walked over to them. "Mind if I join you?"

"Nancy!" Liz cried with her usual enthusiasm. "Of course. What's up?"

Nancy shrugged. "Narrow escape from the library," she explained. She looked at Liz and Daniel again and noticed that they were holding hands.

"I hope you don't mind my saying this," Nancy began, "but it's nice to see you two together again."

Liz blushed. Daniel was grinning like a man who'd just won the lottery.

"Well, I guess you'd have to thank Black and White Nights for that," Liz joked. "I've got a soft spot for men in tuxedos."

"Nah." Daniel smiled. "I was the one missing her. But it was her game-show hostess impersonation that pushed me over the edge."

At least that makes two good things that happened at Black & White Nights, Nancy thought.

"But it's still hard to feel happy about the weekend," Liz admitted. "With the theft and all."

"Speaking of which, what's happening with it?" Daniel asked. "Any leads?"

"Yes," Nancy admitted. "But unfortunately the main suspect is still Paul."

"Why would *anyone* think he did it?" Liz asked for them all.

"Well, he did know the computer code for the lock on the safe, and he was handling all the money, so in the eyes of the police he's the obvious suspect. And then, you know, a witness came forward, so things are looking pretty bad for him," Nancy said.

"I must have missed the witness," Liz said. "Is it someone who saw him take the money?"

"Someone claims to have seen him coming out of the office downstairs with a bag," Nancy explained. "Paul says they were supplies from the storeroom, but since the guy's a friend of Porter's son, everyone believes him."

"One of Sam's friends?" Daniel asked. "Which one?"

"His name is Glenn," Nancy replied. "You know, the one with the dark hair that falls in his face."

"No!" Daniel moaned. "That guy's a total airhead. I don't know why anyone's taking his word for anything. As if he or his blond pal could even find their way out of a paper bag."

"What do you mean?" Nancy asked, suddenly perking up.

"I ran into those two boneheads on Friday night," Daniel said, shaking his head. "The whole event was already over, and they were still wandering around in the basement looking for the bathroom."

"The *bathroom?*" Nancy echoed.

"Yeah, pretty stupid, huh?" Daniel said. "They said someone told them that's where the bathrooms were—in the basement. Right, like in a brand new multifloor theater arts complex, the only bathrooms would be hidden down in the basement. Are they gullible, or what?"

"No," Nancy said. "Actually they aren't the gullible ones. I think we are."

"What do you mean?" Liz asked, suddenly worried.

All along Nancy had felt there was something suspicious about one of Sam's friends being the only witness against Paul. Especially now that she was sure Sam had been cheating at cards.

"That's the same story Glenn gave to Porter and the cops," Nancy explained. "But he said he saw Paul leaving the office on *Saturday* night. And the reason he was down there was because he was looking for the bathroom."

"He really *is* an idiot if he got lost two nights in a row," Daniel muttered.

"Unless he wasn't lost," Nancy replied slowly. "Either time."

CHAPTER 13

"Aren't you hungry yet? It is seven o'clock, after all."

Casey lifted her head over her stack of books of Russian literary criticism. She'd placed them strategically, so she wouldn't have to see Charley stretched out on her bed killing time until she was done with her work. She felt guilty enough running from one thing to another and putting Charley off. He kept saying he had something important to talk about, but he needed a chunk of uninterrupted time to discuss it. But Casey didn't have a chunk of uninterrupted time.

Besides, why couldn't he just wait to talk to her when they went away, during her weekend break? They'd have plenty of "uninterrupted" time on their weekend to go over everything to their heart's content, whatever it was.

"I can't even think about food," she replied. "But if you want to go down to dinner, feel free. I need to finish this paper tonight."

"Maybe I can help you," Charley said, dangling his legs over the side of the bed.

Casey fought back a grin. "Sure, okay. How's your knowledge of Russian peasant life at the turn of the century?"

Charley nodded. "What a coincidence. It's pretty good, as a matter of fact. I was just reading up on it on the plane Friday morning."

Casey and Charley locked eyes, then burst out in laughter. "Wow, do I love you, you big dummy," she said. She dropped her pen, closed her book, and stood.

Charley rose to meet her. "I'm glad you said that," he said, "because I wanted to—"

"Oh, how sweet, another intimate moment." Stephanie drawled sarcastically from the slightly opened door.

She traipsed into the room, loaded down with shopping bags. "Give me a hand, will you, Charley? There are more bags in the lounge."

Casey cringed and shrugged at Charley, who, she could tell, was about to explode. "Charley?" she whispered soothingly. She'd already given him the speech about Stephanie. *She* had to live with her, not him, so he had to be the perfect gentleman, even when Stephanie deserved to be bound and gagged.

"Sure," Charley said through clenched teeth as he stomped out into the hallway.

Casey breathed a sigh of relief. "So what did you buy, Steph?"

"Oh, just a few things," Stephanie said, non-chalantly waving her hand as Charley returned, struggling through the door with five huge shopping bags from different clothing boutiques.

"Whew," Casey gasped, watching Charley collapse under their weight on Stephanie's bed. "What's the occasion?"

"My father's dumb wedding. But just because *I'm* not getting married doesn't mean I shouldn't care about the way I look, does it?"

Casey and Charley exchanged helpless looks. "Of course not," Casey said.

Stephanie started pacing back and forth between the two beds, waving her hands in the air. "And of course he's bringing the little vixen up to visit soon," she ranted. "And how much am I looking forward to that? A big zero. If she thinks for one iota of a second that I'm going to call her Mom," she stated with hatred, "she must think I'm as blind and naive as my father."

Casey folded her arms, listening intently. "So why don't you tell me how you really feel, Steph?" she quipped, hoping a little humor would lighten the mood.

Stephanie groaned loudly. "Marriage is a plague!" she cried.

"Look at it this way," Casey replied reasonably. "If it weren't for marriage, you wouldn't be here."

Stephanie paused, thinking, then waved her hand dismissively. "You don't need marriage for *that*. The only reason this little bratty twenty-eight-year-old is my stepmother is that she doesn't have a life of her own. Marriage is like a vampire. Say bye-bye to your womanhood and your wallet."

In the corner of her eye Casey could see Charley pale and cringe. Casey had to laugh. She could see that Stephanie's rant was an act. Why couldn't Charley?

Poor guy, she thought. He has a lot to learn about human nature.

Bess shifted her feet and adjusted her backpack on her shoulder for about the hundredth time. She was standing outside the Theater Arts building waiting for Nancy to meet her for dinner. Bess's stomach was really grumbling. If Nancy didn't hurry, they wouldn't even have time to make it to the Student Union cafeteria before it closed. It was already eight o'clock and they only had about another half hour.

Just then Bess saw Nancy striding toward her through the darkness.

"Hey, Bess," Nancy said, wrapping her arm around Bess's shoulders in a friendly hug. "How are you holding up?"

Bess shrugged. "I know you're my best friend, but do you really want to hear?"

Nancy grimaced. "If it's that bad, maybe you don't have to tell me everything. Trust me. I can understand how you must feel. This whole thing is eating me up, too. I can hardly think of anything else."

"You know, it's not even me," Bess said. "It's Paul. He's so depressed I can't talk to him." Bess dropped her head on Nancy's shoulder as they began walking through campus together.

"I have a terrible feeling that he's pulling away from me," Bess moaned. "It's bad enough that he's suspected of stealing. He's so embarrassed that he won't even let me near him. But what if he gets in real trouble? What if no one can find the real thieves?"

Bess knew she was working herself up over this, but she couldn't help it. She hadn't been able to comfort Paul. And he certainly wasn't in a position to be able to comfort her. He was terrified of being charged as a criminal.

Bess was so close to crying, she didn't know what to do. She just couldn't believe that such a magical weekend could have turned into such a disaster!

"They're just waiting," Bess said sadly. "If they

can't find anything else, they're just going to charge Paul."

"I don't know about that," Nancy said thoughtfully.

"What do you mean?" Bess asked, the first faint flickerings of hope stirring in her chest. She should have known that Nancy would help. Nancy knew Paul wasn't guilty. Maybe she had a lead on the real thieves.

"Well, the guy who says he saw Paul with a bag says he was in the basement on Saturday night looking for the bathroom," Nancy said. "But Daniel saw this same guy down there Friday night with the same excuse of looking for the bathroom. I, for one, think that's more than a coincidence."

"And just because someone's carrying a bag doesn't mean it's full of money!" Bess snapped. "I hate the way that makes Paul sound."

"You know what, Bess?" Nancy asked. "You're right. Paul said he'd been down to the storeroom *and* the office. Glenn told Porter he saw Paul leaving the office. But how did he know he saw Paul leaving the *office* and not the *storeroom?* Both times Paul would have been carrying the same bag. How would Glenn know which room Paul was leaving?

"And you know what else?" Nancy suddenly added. "I don't know why I didn't think of this before, but remember on Friday night Glenn and Jack were with Sam the whole time?"

"You mean as his personal drink-bearers and back-rubbers?" Bess muttered. "Sure, they were all over him."

"Exactly," Nancy said. "And apparently Glenn and Jack were also there on Saturday night. But did we see them near Sam?"

Bess tried to remember. But the only thing she could picture was Paul's face, crumpled in disappointment and worry. "I'm not sure," Bess admitted. "I don't think so."

"We didn't," Nancy said decisively. "Not until the end, when they came to get him and they all left together. Sam had said that Saturday night was going to be even better than Friday. So where were those guys all night? And why did they all leave early?" Nancy wondered.

"Well, maybe they decided they'd made enough," Bess said, horrified to think what would have happened if Sam had stayed and won even more money. "After all, the only person who made more than they did was whoever stole Friday's proceeds."

All of a sudden Nancy's eyes grew wide.

"Bess, you're right!" Nancy cried. "The thief is the only person who made more than Sam. Unless . . ." Nancy said slowly. "Unless there was more than one thief. And Sam was one of them."

Bess could see that Nancy was excited about something, but she didn't get it.

"How could Sam have stolen anything?" she asked. "He was sitting upstairs all night. We were all watching him."

"Right," Nancy agreed. "He was sitting upstairs all night, winning so much money that we had to watch him. We were all paying attention to Sam, but not to what was going on downstairs in the office."

"Speaking of the office—" Bess cringed, reaching into her purse and pulling out the cuff link she'd found. "I'm sorry I forgot to give this back to you," she began, dropping the shiny object into Nancy's hand. "I've been so distracted by this whole thing. And so worried for Paul."

But Nancy didn't answer at first. She was staring down at her palm, confusion all over her face.

"Uh, Bess," Nancy began hesitantly, "I know you're stressed, but, uh ... I have to tell you, I don't wear a tuxedo."

For the first time in days Bess laughed. "I know that," she replied, waving her hand in Nancy's face. "I'm not a *complete* fool, you know."

Nancy raised a brow.

"Oh, right," Bess chuckled. "I'm not even an incomplete fool. Of course it's not yours. It's Jake's. I found it Saturday night, but after the whole, you know, disaster, I just forgot to give it to him."

"What?" Nancy asked again.

"The cuff link Jake kept losing all night," Bess reminded her. "Remember?"

"I remember that one of his cuff links kept falling out," Nancy agreed. "But Jake returned his tux this morning and he wasn't missing anything. Why did you think this was Jake's?" Nancy asked. "Where did you find it?"

"It was downstairs in the office," Bess explained. "Remember we all went down there together. I figured it had to be Jake's because he was there—"

"Wait a minute!" Nancy interrupted her, leaning forward. "Did you say you found this in the office?"

"Yeah," Bess repeated. "Downstairs."

"In the office where the money was kept?" Nancy asked again. "Where the money was stolen from?"

"I said yes," Bess replied almost irritated. "Where the money was— Oh no!" Suddenly Bess realized what Nancy was saying. "I just thought it was Jake's," she murmured, "because his kept falling off."

"Bess," Nancy said, her eyes bright. "Do you realize what this is?" She held the cuff link out between them. "This is it. This is the clue that's going to nail the thief. Someone lost this in the office. It wasn't Jake. And I doubt it was Paul or

Daniel. If it wasn't any of the Zeta guys, there's only one other person it could be."

"The thief," Bess said softly.

"We've got to find out where this came from," Nancy said. "All the stores are closed, but first thing tomorrow, we've got to go down to the tux place."

Nancy dropped the cuff link into her bag.

"Whoever lost this is going to have some major explaining to do," she said. "And I'm beginning to have a pretty good idea who it might be."

"Hi, Freddy!" Jake said as he and Nancy walked through the door of the tux shop on Tuesday morning.

"You again!" Freddy cried with a scowl. "What do you want now, to complain again? You want a discount or something?"

Jake laughed. "Actually, I just wanted to know if anyone had returned any tuxes with a missing cuff link."

Freddy laughed, his shoulders bobbling up and down. "Not that many. Only about twenty-five!"

Jake groaned.

"That's half of my income, charging for lost cuff links, bow ties, shoelaces, buttons—"

Jake could practically hear the air leave Nancy's mouth. He felt pretty deflated himself. "That's too bad," Jake said despondently. "Because I found one, and I thought you might be able to figure out whose it was."

Freddy held out his strong tailor's hands. "Give it here. I know them all. I have all different kinds. They're like little babies to me."

Jake handed him the cuff link and waited while Freddy examined it. He dropped it on the counter with a ping. "Number fifty-seven," he said with total conviction.

Nancy leaned across the counter, smiling. "You wouldn't happen to know who it was that rented number fifty-seven by any chance, would you?"

Freddy's mouth split in a cheerful grin. "For you, anything," he said, flipping the pages of an old school ledger. "What did this boy do, ask your girl here to dance, behind your back?" he asked while he searched.

Jake shrugged. "In a manner of speaking."

Freddy's finger rested on a name halfway down the page. He raised his eyes. "Friday afternoon he rented. Glenn Hartley."

Jake's eyes widened. "Friday?"

"Glenn!" Nancy exclaimed. "Right! When we saw him Friday night, we remembered him from the shop."

Jake nodded. "This is too weird."

"No, it's not," Nancy said breathlessly. "Listen. He's Sam's friend. And he's also the witness who claimed to see Paul leaving the office with the bag full of money!"

"Money?" Freddy interjected, his eyes narrowed with interest. "This sounds good. What am I missing?"

Jake opened his mouth, then shut it. "It's a long story. "Come on, Nance."

Nancy followed him out. They stopped just outside the door.

"Look, if that's his cuff link," Nancy said, "and Bess found it in the office, then that proves that *he* was in the office *himself*."

Jake nodded. "I got it! He wasn't looking for the bathroom at all that night. It's a good thing Daniel ran into him."

"I just *knew* he was a suspicious witness," Nancy said. "It was right in front of our eyes the *entire* time."

Jake nodded, the entire picture coming into focus. "No wonder the three of them left early Saturday night—"

"Because they'd already made ten times more money than Sam had won by cheating all night!"

Jake shook his head. "Wow. They really had us running in all the wrong directions."

"Until they tripped over Daniel," Nancy added with a sigh.

Jake's heart was racing. They had all the pieces to the puzzle. Now they had to put it together— in front of the right person.

"Wait here," Jake said, and sprinted back to

the store. He ran up to the counter and swiped the cuff link.

"Where are you going with my cuff link?" Freddy cried.

Jake flashed him a thumbs-up. "I'll replace this tomorrow. I promise!"

"Where to now?" he asked Nancy when he returned to the street.

"I think the police station might be the first stop on our tour. Then maybe a little cruise up to the Porter mansion. How does that sound?"

Smiling, Jake cupped her chin and kissed her hard on the lips. "Sounds perfect."

"This isn't such a great idea," Glenn complained as Nancy, Jake, and Bess led him up to Zeta house. "If I go in there, I'll get killed."

"He's right," Nancy said. "Though the only reason I wouldn't want the Zeta guys to have him is because we need him. Bess, go in and get Paul."

While Bess ran in, Jake watched Glenn. Nancy was mulling over the intelligence of Sam's little plan.

I have to admit, it was good, she thought to herself. *It was the perfect diversion. I should have seen it coming.*

"Hey, what's taking them so long?" Glenn snapped.

"Hey, yourself," Jake shot back. "Keep a lid

on it. You're lucky we're giving you the chance to help us out."

Bess led a beaming Paul out.

"She tell you everything?" Nancy asked.

"At about a million miles an hour," Paul replied.

"But you got the picture?" Jake asked.

Paul glared threateningly at Glenn. "Yes."

They all squeezed into Nancy's Mustang and drove out of Weston to the crest of a hill overlooking town. The winding streets held large stately homes with perfectly manicured hedges.

When they reached the Porter residence, a long, gravel driveway led up to a large house with terraced gardens and a tennis court on the side.

"Why would Sam need to steal money?" Jake wondered aloud. "It's obvious his father has money."

"That's what I'd like to know," Paul growled.

"And we're about to find out," Nancy replied.

A housekeeper opened the door.

"We'd like to see Mr. Porter, senior *and* junior," Nancy said firmly.

"Sam junior is upstairs," the housekeeper announced, stepping side.

Nancy caught the glint in Jake's eye. "Good," she said.

They waited in anxious silence in the plush living room for a few minutes. Finally Samuel Porter Sr. came in wearing slippers.

"What's the meaning of this? And what are *you* doing here?" he said, catching sight of Paul. "Get out immediately, or I'll call the police!"

"You don't need to do that, Mr. Porter," Nancy replied. She glanced at her watch. "They should be here in about five minutes. We have some bad news."

Porter shook his head. "What could be worse than approximately fifty thousand dollars missing?"

"Unfortunately . . ." Nancy started to explain, then decided to go slower. She knew the truth was going to hurt Porter. "It's a long story," she said. "But first of all, Paul Cody is innocent."

Porter looked at Glenn. "But, Glenn, didn't you say you witnessed this boy stealing that money with your own eyes?"

Glenn was staring at his shoes.

"Glenn?" Porter prodded him. When Glenn remained silent, Porter turned to Nancy. "So if it wasn't Paul, then who was it?"

Nancy cleared her throat. She was about to tell him when Sam came walking in. "What are you all doing here?" he said, surprised.

"Sam," Porter said. "They say they know who the thief is. Glenn is here with some of the—"

But Porter stopped talking, and Nancy realized he had seen the guilty look that crossed his son's face.

Sam swallowed hard and looked as if he'd been

punched. His cocky posture collapsed for a second. His hands shot into his pockets.

"Will *someone* tell me what this is all about?" Porter roared.

Sam seemed to regain his composure and stared defiantly at Nancy.

"They're all liars, Dad!" he said, walking over to his father. "They just want to get their friend out of trouble."

Porter crossed his arms. "What's going on, Sam?" He looked from his son to Nancy.

"I'm sorry to have to tell you this," Nancy said, then explained how Sam had rigged the blackjack with marked cards, and how that scheme was just a cover for the theft of the money. The life seemed to drain out of Porter as she talked.

"Dad, I told you—" Sam started to say, but his father cut him off.

"How did you get the computer code to the safe, Sam?" Porter stared hard at his son.

Sam was shifting from foot to foot, looking nervously around the room. He finally met his father's gaze. "I stole it, from your office. I was looking for the keys to the Jag in your desk drawer, and I found the manufacturer's booklet that came with the safe. You'd written the code on the back. You always have had a lousy memory." Sam paused for breath, then continued.

Nancy noticed he was starting to lose his cool as he talked.

"I heard you on the phone the next day with him." Sam indicated Paul. "You were talking about the charity thing and about using the safe to hold the proceeds. It seemed like an easy gig."

Sam looked around the room at everyone staring at him, and suddenly became panicked. "Do something, Dad!" he cried.

But Porter took a step back. "I can't do anything for you now, son," he said, his voice thick with emotion.

Nancy could see the disappointment and humiliation in his eyes.

"That's the whole problem!" Sam shrieked. "You've never done anything for me. You blow five hundred dollars for charity, but you never even give your own son an extra dime! Why do you think I wanted the money?"

"Sam," Porter beseeched his son. "What did you do with the money?"

Sam's face twisted in an ugly sneer. "You'll get all your money," he spat. "I have every dime of your precious dirty money in my room."

Sam, glowering, sat down in a chair.

Porter turned to Paul, struggling to speak. He looked like a broken man.

"Of course you will accept my apologies for accusing you," he said.

Paul nodded and said, "I was still careless with Friday's earnings, Mr. Porter," Paul said. "I'm sorry."

"Not nearly as sorry as I am," Porter said sadly.

"And the least I can do," Porter continued, "besides helping my son, of course, is to give the money I provided to set up the casino to the charities and campus groups, and then to double it as my personal contribution."

The entire room seemed to sigh with relief. Everyone was too preoccupied to speak.

"I'm sure the kids in Helping Hands," Paul finally spoke up, "would want to thank you." Nancy nodded enthusiastically.

Outside, police cars were pulling into the driveway. Porter looked sadly at his son. "Come on, Sam, you have some money to return."

CHAPTER 14

"Hey," Bess said, sidling up to Paul in her room that night. "Had enough excitement this week?"

"Enough to last a lifetime," Paul replied, a little horrified.

Bess smiled happily and wrapped her arms around Paul. All she wanted to do was disappear with him for days and days. . . .

Exams, a little voice poked at her from deep inside her brain.

"See, everything works out," she said brightly. "The charities got their money and I got you back."

"And Sam, Glenn, and Jack got a personalized tour of the inside of a jailhouse," Paul said. He looked down at her. "I think we need to spend a lot more time together, that's what I think."

Bess collapsed against him. "You have no idea how badly I needed to hear that."

"But I decided one more thing, too," Paul said seriously. "That I'll never ever, ever, *ever* get involved in something like this again."

"Ever?" Bess asked, bracing herself.

Paul let out a laugh, "Ever!"

"No more working together?" Bess teased. "We don't want to have to go back to the 'Working Woman's Datebook,' do we?" she asked.

Paul smiled and blushed at the mention of the datebook he'd given her. When they'd first met, Bess had been too busy with her sorority, schoolwork, and the theater department to find the time for a date with him. So he'd given her the datebook, complete with times for him penciled into her weekly schedule.

"Maybe your next charity should be me," Paul suggested, his eyes gleaming.

Bess put her arms around his neck, pulling him close. "Very good idea."

Paul looked into Bess's eyes. "Let's start work on that charity right now."

"The sooner the better," Bess said as she brought her lips up to meet his.

Passing under the streetlight on the campus quad, Reva held up her wrist, letting her new gold charm bracelet play in the light. It was close to midnight. She smiled. It was so easy to lose track of time when she was with Andy. In fact, sometimes she wondered what it would be like if she didn't have to go back to her room at all.

What if we were the only people in the world? Reva thought dreamily as she made her way down the walk through the middle of campus. What if time didn't matter at all?

She was on her way back to her dorm after a late "study" session at Andy's. Supposedly, they were going to be studying for the upcoming exams. But somehow, their "studying" didn't get very far. In fact, their textbooks were barely opened. She'd walked into his room to find candles burning on the coffee table and soft music playing. It had been their most romantic evening yet. And as soon as she left his apartment, Reva couldn't wait to see him the next day.

Maybe you're falling in love, she told herself.

"In love?" she murmured out loud, just to see how it sounded.

Reva smiled again and reached for her wrist, touching the beautiful gold bracelet Andy had given her on Saturday night, with the lovely heart charm and the *R* engraved in the center. *R*—for Reva, for Ross, for Rodriguez. Reva decided it was the most beautiful piece of jewelry she'd ever owned.

Reva heard a twig snap behind her.

She turned around. "Hello?" she called.

No answer.

"That's weird."

The night was silent. The pathways cutting between the grass were mostly empty except for a few stray students, like Reva, returning to a dorm or apartment. Reva looked around, taking in the emptiness for the first time. She had to admit that she was getting a little uncomfortable.

The darkened buildings loomed above her. She often left the computer lab this late and walked home alone without a problem. But tonight she felt weird. Maybe it was the wind. The swaying trees sounded alive and mean.

"You're just hearing things," she said, lowering her head and cutting into an alleyway, a shortcut that sliced the walk in half.

But there was that sound again!

"Hello?" she called, this time a little fearfully. "Is anybody there?"

She squinted and looked into the dark, but it was like peering into a lightless tunnel. She turned and quickened her pace.

Up ahead, she could see the lights of Thayer Hall. She breathed a sigh of relief and slowed down.

But before she walked out of the alleyway onto the main walkway, she felt herself being slammed up against the wall.

"What . . . ?"

Then she felt a strong hand holding her up against the wall, and someone's rapid breathing.

Her backpack was yanked off. It caught on the bracelet, and she felt another hand rip the thin gold chain from her wrist. She was pulled backward and pushed to the ground, hitting her head slightly against the concrete. Stunned, it took Reva a moment to recover and turn over. She heard footsteps running off as she sat up.

Reva was alone. At first she couldn't see anything. After standing, she walked forward, and up ahead in the gloomy darkness she made out the big square shape of her backpack, with other black shapes scattered beside it.

"My books," she whispered.

Reva walked to her bag. The small side pocket was ripped open and her wallet was gone.

Reva reached out to grab one of her notebooks, lying open on the grass, and even though it was dark, she suddenly saw that her wrist was bare.

Her bracelet was gone, too.

She dropped the notebook and brought her wrist closer to her face. She pressed it against her forehead for a moment, then brought her arms into her chest and bent over.

She started shaking, then sobbing uncontrollably.

Nancy was walking across campus, her books hugged to her chest, the cool autumn breeze fingering her strawberry blond hair. She'd just gotten out of her first Wednesday morning class, Journalism 101, with her favorite professor, Dan McCall, and was in a great mood.

"You've got to stop smiling at total strangers!" she chided herself.

"Nancy!"

She whirled around as Jake fell into step beside her.

"Where are you going?" he asked.

"I'm meeting George in about half an hour at my dorm. Where are *you* going?" she replied.

"Wherever *you're* going," he said.

Nancy nodded. "Good answer. You win the jackpot. A cup of coffee with me before I go to see George."

They each got a coffee to go at Java Joe's and sat with them on the grass in the morning sunshine. "Guess what?" she asked.

Jake narrowed his eyes with concentration. "Is it bigger than a bread box?"

Nancy laughed. "Barely."

"Animal, vegetable, or mineral?"

"Animal, most definitely. Helping Hands called me first thing this morning—"

Jake gasped. "You were paired with your little sister!"

Nancy nodded excitedly.

"Excellent!" Jake was saying. "What's her name?"

"Anna Pederson. She's twelve. I'm so psyched.

Trips to the mall. And movies. And maybe I'll take her to some of the concerts and football games on campus—"

Jake was laughing. "Whoa, hold on! Aren't you only supposed to spend two hours a week with her?"

Nancy shrugged. "Yes, but how do you start a relationship at two hours a week? What if I told *you* we could only spend two hours a week together?"

Jake took Nancy's coffee and put it in the grass. Then he slid over and took her around the waist. "First I'd kidnap you," he whispered, nuzzling her neck, "then I'd charter a private plane and take you away."

Nancy pushed him away playfully. "Then you see my point."

"The only point I see is the tip of your very beautiful nose, and I want that point to come to me."

Nancy leaned over and softly kissed his neck, his chin, each cheek, and then, very, very softly, the tip of his nose. Jake, with a sigh, leaned down and kissed her lips.

Casey felt as if a weight had been lifted from her shoulders. She'd finally dropped off her big Russian lit paper early that morning. Now she was rushing back to the dorm as fast as she could. Casey checked her watch as she hurried up the stairs to the suite. Charley's plane was leaving in just over an hour.

Her heart was pounding. She hadn't told him what she did. Last night, after Charley went back to his motel, she had taken the peroxide hair dye that she'd bought earlier and slipped into the bathroom. Everyone else might have thought she was kidding when she said she liked the way she looked in a blond wig. But she wasn't. An hour later she had emerged a blond!

Unfortunately, most of her suitemates had been less than thrilled at her transformation. But some of her classmates in Russian lit had complimented her on her new look. She was torn about whether to keep it, so she was eager to get Charley's reaction. If he loved the color, it stayed.

Casey flung open the door to her room. Charley was standing by her bed, with a bag slung over his shoulder.

She dropped her bookbag by the door and strode over to Charley, pushing his bag off his shoulder and wrapping his arms around her.

But Charley's mouth was open, and his eyes were aimed above hers. "What . . . did . . . you *DO!*" he cried.

Casey stepped back and struck a pose. "You like? I love it." She stepped in front of the mirror and tilted her head one way, then the other, admiring the bleached white hair.

"You'll get used to it," she said blithely.

Charley was shaking his head. "I don't think so, Case," he said.

"But my Russian lit class liked it," Casey said, disappointed.

Charley winced. "They were being nice."

Casey pursed her lips. "You *really* don't like it? Even a little bit?" She sighed, burying her face in his neck.

She closed her eyes as Charley ran his fingers through her hair. "I can't believe you really did this," he said in disbelief.

Casey raised her eyebrows. "I'm getting daring in my old age."

"But your red hair was so beautiful," Charley said. "It was famous. It was so *you.*"

"I'm *bored* with me," she started to explain.

"I'm not," Charley said meaningfully.

Casey looked at him, nodding. "Okay," she said, disappointed. "I'll dye it back. My suitemates didn't think it was so great, either. Now, let's have a proper goodbye kiss."

Casey was waiting for Charley to plant one of his wonderfully wicked kisses on her lips, but instead, she felt him stiffen a little in her arms.

"Is something wrong?" she asked. "I mean, besides the hair?"

"I don't know," Charley admitted, his eyes drifting from the top of her head to her eyes. "Well, yes, actually there is."

"What?" she whispered.

"To tell you the truth," Charley continued, "this isn't what I planned at all."

Casey looked puzzled.

"We're actually finally alone," Charley moaned. "For the first time since I've been here, we have a quiet, uninterrupted moment together."

"So," Casey said, stepping back again and looking at him. "You wanted to talk about something. What's wrong with now? Let's talk."

"Oh, Casey." Charley sighed, dropping onto the bed. "I have to leave for the airport in fifteen minutes. And there's no way I can stay here even one more day. This wasn't how I wanted to do this," he said.

"Charley?" Casey said softly. "You're scaring me."

He's trying to break up with me, she suddenly realized. That's why he's been looking so thoughtful and pensive all weekend. That's why he's been upset every time I put off our "conversation." Because he's a nice guy he didn't want to drop the bombshell and duck out the door.

"Casey," Charley began slowly. "I've been thinking about this for a long time. More so, I guess since you've started school. But"—he shook his head—"I really wanted to do this the right way."

I've started school, Casey thought. I'm far

away. There must be other women asking him out.

I can't believe it's over, she thought.

"Casey?" Charley was saying. He held out his hand for her, and she walked toward him, feeling sick to her stomach.

"Casey, I hope you won't be surprised at what I want to say," Charley said. "I hope you've been feeling it yourself, too."

Charley took her hands in his and brought them slowly to his lips. He reached into his pocket and brought out his cupped fist. Then he opened one of her hands and pressed something into it.

Casey looked down.

There, on her right palm, was a ring.

It was the most beautiful ring she'd ever seen. The diamond was an elegant pinpoint of pure, clear light set in a simple pool of gold.

"Casey?" Charley asked, catching her eyes. "Casey Fontaine," he whispered, "will you marry me?"

NEXT IN NANCY DREW ON CAMPUS™:

Andy Rodriguez has given Nancy's suitemate Reva a token of his love—a bracelet with a gold charm. But Reva's life is anything but charmed. She's been mugged, and the incident has the entire campus on edge. Nancy suspects that there's more to the crime than meets the eye. She's determined to break the story and make sure the whole truth comes out.

Casey, meanwhile, is facing her own moment of truth. Her boyfriend, TV heartthrob Charley Stern, has proposed marriage, but on one condition—that she leave Wilder. Love has always been a risky business, but lately, as Nancy's about to discover, if you fall for the "wrong" person, there are those who will go out of their way to cut you down ... in *In the Name of Love*, Nancy Drew on Campus #11.

Now your younger brothers or sisters can take a walk down Fear Street....

R·L·STINE'S
GHOSTS of FEAR STREET ®

1 **Hide and Shriek** 52941-2/$3.99

2 **Who's Been Sleeping in My Grave?**
52942-0/$3.99

3 **Attack of the Aqua Apes** 52943-9/$3.99

4 **Nightmare in 3-D** 52944-7/$3.99

5 **Stay Away From the Treehouse**
52945-5/$3.99

6 **Eye of the Fortuneteller** 52946-3/$3.99

7 **Fright Knight** 52947-1/$3.99

8 **The Ooze** 52948-X/$3.99

9 **Revenge of the Shadow People**
52949-8/$3.99

 A MINSTREL® BOOK
Published by Pocket Books